Born to Lead

2017 *Pam Jackson* enjoy!

Born to Lead

To Janis

 Veni

Pam Jackson

Copyright © 2017 by Pam Jackson.

Library of Congress Control Number:		2017911133
ISBN:	Hardcover	978-1-5434-3694-5
	Softcover	978-1-5434-3693-8
	eBook	978-1-5434-3692-1

All rights reserved. No part of this book may be reproduced or transmitted in any form or by any means, electronic or mechanical, including photocopying, recording, or by any information storage and retrieval system, without permission in writing from the copyright owner.

This is a work of fiction. Names, characters, places and incidents either are the product of the author's imagination or are used fictitiously, and any resemblance to any actual persons, living or dead, events, or locales is entirely coincidental.

Any people depicted in stock imagery provided by Thinkstock are models, and such images are being used for illustrative purposes only.
Certain stock imagery © Thinkstock.

Print information available on the last page.

Rev. date: 08/28/2017

To order additional copies of this book, contact:
Xlibris
1-888-795-4274
www.Xlibris.com
Orders@Xlibris.com
757081

CONTENTS

Acknowledgments ix

Introduction xiii

Home! 1

Hollywood 23

Back to Reality 31

My Run for President! 68

MOM'S VACATION!! 73

My Herding Career! 94

Dad's Leg Was Stolen 114

"Dear Veni" Letters 123

My Run for Mayor! 142

To my standard poodle, Charley, who was a "soul mate" dog.
You went to the Poodle Palace in 2008, and I still miss you.
And yes, your collar will remain in my car for the rest of my life.

Acknowledgments

To my husband, who has been through more than one person should have to endure. So many surgeries, but he still keeps a smile on his face and a positive attitude. We all love you in the Jackson household, Demi, Levi, Veni, and me!

Born to Lead

Jail Time!

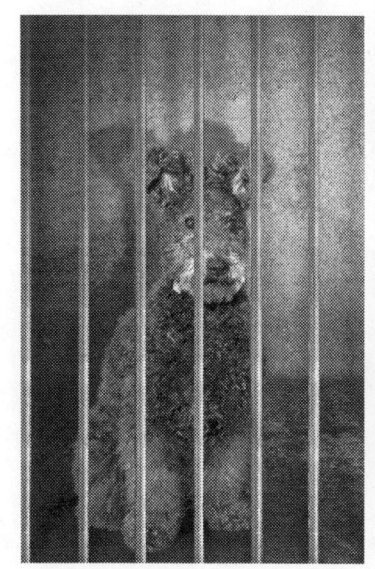 

Introduction

As the jail doors clanged, the horrible truth hit them. This would be their home for the next six months: county jail!

We could not afford a good attorney, so a basset hound attorney took our case. He had just graduated from law school, and we think he cheated on his bar exam. Six months for Demi for driving without a license and to Levi and me for being conspirators—mostly me, they say. Sniff! Sniff!

Letter 1

Yes, Demi, Levi, and I got six months of jail time because someone from the government intercepted my e-mail to my boyfriend, Hoover. We all cried and asked for leniency, but they refused. They said we were bad doggies and probably should have been sentenced to more than six months! *Just for driving without a license?* Demi was the driver, for heaven's sake.

"Why did Levi and I have to go to jail?" I asked.

The judge told me it was because it was my idea.

Oh please! I told the judge that Demi just laid around all day anyway, but Levi and I were herding breeds and we *needed* to be busy, so it would be very difficult for us to sit in a jail cell.

You know what she said? "That is good because you will be cleaning toilets all day long."

This was a nightmare! I said, "Please, Mom and Dad, we need to be bailed out. I know you are poor, but could you ask for a loan?"

They replied, "No!"

Veni

Letter 2

To all of Veni's friends,

The first phone call!

I had exactly two minutes to talk to Veni, Levi, and Demi separately. Veni cried the whole time because she was in a cell all by herself. I told her to be brave. She was thinking about chewing through her cell so she could be with Demi and Levi, but I said, "No!"

The guards were not nice. They told her she was a brat and deserved jail time. As a matter of fact, if she did not clean the toilets, help cook, clean the floors, and do dishes, they would recommend she stay longer than six months.

Levi and Demi were much braver because they were together. The guards—two pit bulls named Tank and Coop—were much nicer to them. Levi said they were actually flirting with Demi." Not a surprise," I said to Levi. I told Levi to watch after her!

Levi mentioned that he got a call from a *very* famous dog attorney! *And* he was known to be one of the smartest. He is a border collie named Johnny Collieran. He had studied under Johnny Cochran (OJ Simpson's attorney). He told Levi that he wanted to appeal their trial pro bono! He said he would see the three of them in a week or two.

This is a positive addition to their case.

I am feeling a little better about our three doggies. I know they all have their problems, but we miss them, despite their faults! And I have to admit they have plenty of faults. There will be *new rules* when they arrive home!

Mom

PS: The wine is flowing at our house! It is so peaceful and quiet!

Coop

Tank

Letter 3

Veni,

I think your dogs are in trouble because this time the glove fits.

Hoover

Letter 4

Dear Chris and Shawn,

I received a call from Veni, Levi, and Demi's new attorney, Johnny Collieran. He is asking if there is anything unseemly in the background of our other two children, Chris and Shawn Jackson. Do not worry, boys. I told a little white lie. "Ummm," I told him, "no." I know that he will be checking, so you two had better cover your tracks! Get your high school and college records fast!

I have received a call every day from the two girls and Levi. They want out of jail! They are afraid, and their food is the cheapest dog food the jailers could find. All three have had a few stomach issues. Veni misses her apples! Of course, she complains the most. She does not think it's fair she is by herself in a cell. They are making them read books about how to be good dogs and how not to go the way of the hardened criminals.

Johnny has talked to all three dogs. Demi told him that Veni talked her into driving, and she agreed only because Veni promised to do her chores. She wishes she had not fallen for Veni's tricks. She says she knows (in hindsight) that Veni would not have done her chores anyway. She would come up with some excuse. Levi went along because down deep, he wanted to see some sheep.

Veni told Johnny that she was still very angry with Levi! After all, if she was going to jail, she at least could have spent time with Clint and his sheep—mostly Clint. She is also disturbed with the US government. How dare they intercept her e-mail! It was none of their business, she says.

Johnny does agree, so he will work on this premise.

He will get back to me soon. He is going to speak to the prosecuting attorney, Marsha Clerk. He is hoping she is a basset hound. It is not that they are bad dogs. They are just a little slow.

Mom

Letter 5

Dear Mom and Dad,

All of my friends forgot about my birthday! I turned two years of age (you can tell all of my friends) on September 10. And I spent my birthday in the county jail. Thank you so much, Mom, for bringing me an apple cake along with some green apples from the apple tree!

And it was so nice of you to think about my guards. That extra cake you took them put a star on my report card in prison.

My birthday wish is to be home in a week or two. I trust our attorney, but I wish he would be a little more aggressive. He has too many cases! He tells me that he goes to herding trials. I miss my boyfriend, Clint! I did not want to hear that he was having such a good time. Not fair. Get to work for *me,* Johnny!

I love and miss all my friends, but you *forgot* my birthday. Tears!

Send this on, Mom.

Veni

Letter 6

Dear Mom,

I was resting in my cell when I heard the key open the door. I was excited because I *thought* it was Johnny Collieran with some good news about our case. I was surprised to see a scruffy-looking little dog walk into my cell. The guard introduced me to Frances, the Chihuahua. He told me that she is my new cellmate. Little did I know she is a murderer! The prisons are so full that they sent her to county jail. Lucky me!

She is very tiny and has a weird accent. When she finally decided to talk, she told me the story! She killed her husband, who was also a Chihuahua. His name was Pedro.

She said that she caught him in an affair with a German shepherd. She found him on a ladder kissing and—umm—more! She told him to get the heck (I do not want to say what she *really* said) off the ladder, or she was going to kill him. He did not—*could not,* or so he said—so then she climbed the ladder, grabbed him by his neck, and threw him to the ground. On his way down, which was a long way, he told her he was sorry, and it was just the heat of the moment. These were his last words.

Frances said she can hardly wait to get out of jail because she wants to "look up" that German shepherd.

She did admit that she has a hot temper because she is Latina. If I were the German shepherd, I would be heading back to Germany. I am trying to be on my best behavior, Mom! This may be a problem for me!

Frances is complaining because there is no Mexican food in county jail. She is growling at the guards, Tank and Coop, who have just about had it with her. I am afraid there is going to be a riot.

Why did they put me in a cell by myself? Levi and Demi (especially) have no worries. Demi is still flipping those false eyelashes at the guards. They take her extra snacks. I really do not like her much, but I would take her over Frances.

Our attorney, Johnny, called and said he would be here next week. He is fighting with the government and having meetings with Marsha Clerk. He said that she is a jerk! She thinks that we should have *more* jail time.

Depressed!

Love,

Veni

(Levi and Demi send their love!)

PS: When Johnny comes to see us, I am going to see if he can help Frances move on to prison.

Letter 7

This is the last report from Veni.

Veni called to tell me that she, Demi, and Levi had a visit from Johnny Collieran. Johnny decided to add an attorney by the name of Christopher Doxie to his team. Johnny told them that he is still waiting to get a call back from the government. They will not answer his phone calls or e-mails, even after he left a message that he was going to sue them for over a million dollars. Veni was excited about the million dollars! She said she could replace the rugs, bedspread, and chairs and have enough money to buy her own car. She wants to be able to drive herself to herding practice. She plans on getting her driver's license as soon as she gets out of jail. She refuses to take Levi and does not want Demi to drive. Demi spends too much time looking at herself in the mirror when she is driving, she says!

She also said that she would have enough money to get her dating service going. She wants to find a handsome dog for herself! She is still in love with Clint but thinks perhaps *two* men could be fun! She hopes Clint might be jealous enough to get rid of the wife and dogs?! She is also looking for a boy dog for Demi! She wants Demi out of the house for good. She is so tired of the mirrors, the false eyelashes, and the flirting. Maybe she will marry one of the pit bull guards that she flirts with every day.

Veni thanked me for the leather and the beads. She loves her new collar she made for herself. She says that she loves to bead! She uses her paws and her teeth. Levi and Demi already have nice collars, so she is not making them one. She offered to make one for the guards, but they declined! They told her that they did not want "sissy" collars. She was not happy because she thought they might take her extra food if she did something nice for them. I told her that I would take them another apple cake.

I will keep you informed when I receive another call.

Mom

PS: Veni says that she is worried because her cell mate is flirting with Levi. She is afraid Levi is falling for her petite figure and her accent! She wants me to get to jail ASAP to have a little talk with Levi. She said that she told him to *stay away* from a girl dog that is a murderer for heaven's sake! Geez!

Letter 8

It has been a month now since Demi, Levi and I have been in county jail. They are just now allowing us to write. They do not check our letters going out, just letters coming in. Consequently, I have to tell you a little story about Levi. It has been the most difficult on Levi because he is such a mommy's boy. He cries and moans every night. For those of you who really know Levi, you will understand what I am about to tell you.

Levi met an Irish wolfhound in jail. O'Riley is in for fighting an Irish setter. They were at a pub, and both had a bit too much to drink. O'Riley really is a great guy, but when he drinks, he gets confrontational. He and Levi became friends. They play poker every day and do a lot of talking. They came up with a plan! This had to be done during the day. They waited until the guards went in for a smoke. They had to do this quickly! Levi got on top of O'Riley, crawled up on top of his head, and tried to jump over the fence (he is a *great jumper*). He jumped up *so* high that O'Riley was sure he was going to make it—*but* his coat got caught in the wire, so he was just *hanging* there! O'Riley panicked! He put his big paws up, stretched as far as he could go, and untangled Levi. He later said that it was like trying to pull a spider off a web! He got Levi off the fence just in the nick of time. The guards came out just as O'Riley put Levi on the floor. Whew! It would have been solitary confinement, and two more months in jail! I told Levi to man up and never try anything so stupid again. Mom! Please come and visit a little more often!

And then there is Demi! Because she is on antidepressants, she is handling the jail thing just fine. She spends her time combing her hair and applying her makeup. She traded some makeup with her friend (a golden retriever), and in turn, she got some false eyelashes. I saw her batting her new eyelashes at one of the guards. Disgusting!

I have to go. They only allow us a little time to write, but I will tell you later about *my* new cell mate. *Ugh*!

Love,

Veni

Letter 9

To all *my* friends,

I know you have heard from Veni and Levi about their experience in county jail, but you have not heard my side of the story.

Veni told you that I was flirting with the two pit bull guards, Tank and Coop. Not true! They both flirted with me! They called me their "beautiful lady" every day when they let me out of my cell. They followed me everywhere I went. I heard them fighting over me and yelling at each other. Tank thought that I should be his. Coop disagreed, saying that I was more attracted to him. I was frightened every day that I was jailed. Veni has been telling you lies. She was jealous that they did not find her beautiful!

Veni neglected to tell you what happened to her cell mate, Frances, the Chihuahua. Frances, as you know, has quite a temper. She started bad-mouthing Tank and Coop. They heard her, so Tank grabbed her by the scruff of her neck to take into solitary confinement. She bit him on his cheek as hard as she could! He screamed and dropped her on her head. She was hurt! The words that came out of her mouth cannot be repeated. They were both taken to the hospital. Frances has not been quite right since, and Tank has a permanent scar—kind of like Hoover the lab, as you might remember. Frances's family has hired Johnny Collieran, who is going to sue the county jail.

Love,

Demi

Tank was still in the hospital when we got out of jail, thanks to our great attorney, Johnny. When he found out I was gone, he looked up my address and came to our house. He wanted me to marry him, but I had to tell him no! He got very angry and threatened me. If he could not have me, no other boy dog will either! I was shaking, and Dad told him to leave the house and never come back. He lifted his lip (only one side would lift!), and growled at my dad. He told my dad that he would be back. Dad called 911. Tank ran!

Home!

Letter 10

Hi, friends!

Our attorney, Johnny Collieran is brilliant! With the help of his assistant attorney, Christopher Doxie, *we are free*! He frightened the government with his million-dollar law suit. Their attorney had to admit that they broke into my e-mails. This is against the law.

They settled for five hundred thousand dollars. We are all so happy! I will get a car, Demi wants to go into the beauty business on the shopping channel for dogs, and Levi… Levi just wants Mom!

Mom and Dad picked us up from the county jail today, September 29. I was so excited! I was certain that there would be a party for us. But I was wrong. Mom picked us up in her old car that has three hundred thousand miles and is twelve years old. She was happy to see us but felt that we should be in trouble for taking her car without permission. Demi did not have a license, Levi should have known better, and I should have thought about the fact that her car was *old*! Like her?

After dinner, Mom told us that the check was going to be made out to *her*! Oh no! No car for me and no beauty business for Demi. She told us that *she* will get a new car, new rugs, new bedspread (maybe two), new chairs, and a new couch. The remaining sum will go into savings.

She said that she still does not trust *me*! She feels that I may still destroy the house. She thinks that she may have to replace the *whole* house, and that five hundred thousand will probably not be enough. Dad agrees!

We are very tired—all the stress! But next week, I get to see Clint! Yes. And then Mom tells me that I have to start agility. I should have stayed in jail…

Love,

Veni

Letter 11

Veni, I am so glad that the three of you are out of jail. It has been so long! Please make sure that you mind your manners. Hopefully you know what happens if you do not behave. Sorry about not having a homecoming party. But stay focused on the big picture: you need to make some money now that your mom has taken away what supposed to be yours. I really think that the dog dating service would serve well. My sister Stella has come home to live. I would really like her to be out of my hair. If you could find a doggie date for her, I would be forever grateful!

Your friend,

Willow

PS: My mom says to wish Aunt Demi a belated happy birthday on October 6. She is seven years old now. Maybe that is why she is so grumpy.

PPS: We are having to listen to the same screaming around here as well. We just do not pay attention anymore. I would love my sister to hook up with a pit bull. She tries to beat me up because she is a bit bigger. But I give it right back to her and more. My mom has kept us separated for the last several months. I would really like to put a bully beat down on my sister, Stella. However, we are so well behaved in the house and get along well there. As for the Giants toy, my mom thinks she is a jinx. Let us wait until the Giants win the World Series. If that happens, I would love to give that toy to my folks! Poor Aunt Demi, let me know how her makeover goes. It is so kind of you Veni to do this for Demi.

Letter 12

Dear Willow,

Thanks so much for your advice! Demi has met many pit bull guards. I know Stella will be interested! As soon as I got home, guess what happened!? The 49er football game was on that weekend! The grandkids could not come, but I had to listen to my two brothers, Chris and Shawn (and Dad) yell *very loud! And then*, I had to listen to the San Francisco Giants! They won! Dad called Chris and Shawn *right away*! I do not know *what* makes them so excited about these games, but I even heard Mom yell, "*Go, go, go,*" when the 49er game was on. I am still trying to understand people in the United States.

Love,

Veni

PS: I remembered Demi's birthday. I gave her a gift certificate to the beauty shop. She really needs to do something about her gray muzzle. She flirts with all the boy dogs, but they pay no attention. They think she is old (which she is!). I am looking for an older boy dog for her. It will be a good way to finally get rid of her!

PPS: I have saved the Giants toy for you. Do you want it?

Letter 13

Hi, all!

First and foremost, I would like to say that we are *so* glad to be home. There is nothing like a dog's own bed. In this case, it is Mom and Dad's bed. I heard Mom tell Dad that she is not sleeping well. She said that she has no room to stretch out! She told him that she really did enjoy her vacation from Demi, Veni, and me. She could actually stretch her legs *straight* out and could turn her head without touching Veni's cold nose and the smell of her breath. She would open her eyes briefly, and would be staring into those round, big black eyes—Veni! Veni always has a big smile on her face. Time to get *out* of bed, Mom!

Mom was not feeling well last Saturday, so she had to tell Veni that she could not go to herding practice. If you could only see the look on that spoiled brat's face! She did not speak to any of us, especially Mom. Demi and I got into bed with Mom to take care of her. What did Veni do? She found the loudest squeak toy and squeaked it as *loud* as she could. She got Mom out of bed, all right. Mom put the toy in a cabinet and closed the door, and put a lock on it! She also put Veni in her crate. Poor Veni. Ha!

Veni had the gall to ask Mom and Dad for a motorcycle for Christmas! She thought she was being nice because she did not ask for a car. Didn't she learn anything from jail time? She is convinced that she can get a driver's license! Anything for Mr. Clint…

Every morning Veni starts the chase game with me in Mom and Dad's bedroom. We run a hundred miles an hour… until Mom yells to *stop*! When we get tired, I get a drink of water, and then Veni goes to the bowl, drinks, then stirs the water with her paws, and gets it all over the floor. This is a new thing. She never did this until we got home from jail. I think that she really does enjoy "stirring the pot'!

Levi

Letter 14

Mr. Clint,

Can I come for herding practice? I know that you are not happy with me after I jumped the fence and started chasing the sheep. I also know that you had to throw a net over me to catch me, but I implore that you give me a second chance! I can add a little white to my coat so I look like a Border Collie! I can do freestyle dance. I might be able to do the work all by myself.

Levi

PS: Demi wants to know if she can do herding. I am still laughing!

Letter 15

To all of Demi's friends,

I just wanted to inform you the news about Tank. As you remember, Tank was on the run from the police. Well, Tank hitched some rides from several different people. His scar is on his right side, so when he turned to talk to the nice people who gave him a ride, they quickly found a reason to drop him off when they saw the scar. It is a scar that most dogs and human people do not forget.

He finally made it to Fresno County. He found the only dog bar in town and walked in. He sat down on a barstool. An old beagle named Hector came over to ask him what he would like to drink. He ordered a beer. He sat at the bar with his head hanging low, feeling very sorry for himself. He was a wanted dog and had an ugly scar. Soon, an old gentlemen Labrador retriever farmer walked in and sat next to him.

The beagle, Hector, said to Ted, the Labrador, "The usual?"

Hector said, "Yes, thank you."

Ted was a very friendly guy, so he told Hector to give Tank another beer. They talked about farming and the fact that there was a drought, so it had not been a good year. They sipped their beer and talked some more. Ted asked no questions about Tank. He had the feeling that Tank did not want to talk about himself. After the third beer, Tank asked Ted if he could use his cell phone.

Tank called Coop. He told him where he was. Coop said not to go anywhere. He would be there as quickly as he could. Coop threw on his helmet, jumped on his motorcycle, and was on his way! Tank waited. There were many dogs at the bar, and a beautiful girl dog was singing. Dogs were smoking and drinking. It was sultry and smoky. Ted had left a while ago, so Tank was sitting at the bar by himself feeling bad again. He was now drinking water waiting for Coop.

Three hours later, Coop walked in. They were very good friends, so Coop was worried. He sat down by Tank and told him that he just had to turn himself in. They talked and talked. Tank told Coop that he had *no* self-esteem because of his ugly scar, and this was perhaps the reason that he went after Demi, the poodle.

Just as they were getting up to leave, a young, pretty girl dog came over to talk. She told Tank that her sister thought that he was very handsome and would like to meet him. She loved a dog with a scar. She thought it was very sexy! All of a sudden, the beautiful girl who was singing some sultry love songs walked over. She wore a sequin gown with a plunging neckline and very high heels. She also wore a boa around her neck. She was a knockout! She said to Tank, "Hi, my name is Stella".

Willow, Stella's sister, asked Coop if he would like to come to her table with all her friends. This gave Tank and Stella time to talk. He told her the whole story. She told him that she liked bad boys, and his scar reminded her of Johnny Depp in *Pirates of the Caribbean*. She also told him that he should turn himself in, and she would come visit him a lot.

Soon he was on his way on the back of Coop's motorcycle. He turned himself in. Because he came back, they gave him six months in the county jail. Stella was true to her word. She visited many times, and there was talk of wedding bells. He did tell Stella that Demi was too stuck up (told you!), so he was glad to get rid of her. And by the way, Willow will be happy to get rid of Stella. They do not get along! And did I mention that they are standard poodles?

Demi came home the very day that Tank went back to jail. Too bad! It was so nice without her!

Love,

Veni

PS: I am not too sure if Stella's parents are happy about Stella marrying a felon! And Stella told Tank that he would have a job after his stint in jail. He would be their bouncer at the dog bar. And after Hector retires, he can take his position at bartender/bouncer.

Letter 16

Now an update about Frances, the Chihuahua! As you remember, our wonderful attorney, Johnny Collieran, took over Frances's case. Frances was not quite right after being dropped on her head by Tank. One day after she had been in the hospital for a couple of weeks, she opened her eyes, looked around, and yelled at the top of her lungs, "*Where am I?*" All the nurses and the doctor ran in. Frances was back!

While Johnny was working on her case with the county jail, he decided to look at her original murder case. He appealed after reading about the whole case. Frances wanted everyone to think that she threw her husband, Pedro, off the ladder, but in fact, he *fell*!

He not only won on the county jail case for $100,000 but won the appeal! There was one condition. She had to do community service. You will *never* guess where! She has to be a guard at the county jail! They knew that she was a spitfire, so she could take care of any of the prisoners without a doubt. She started work the same week that Tank went back to jail. All the prisoners cower in the corner when she walks by, except for Tank. He lifts the only side of his lip that will lift and growls!

Letter 17

Dear friends,

This is my second Thanksgiving in America. I still do not get it! Thanksgiving is for giving, not taking! I am in charge of the turkey protest.

Many of my friends are turkeys. They feel (along with me) that they should not sacrificed for the celebration! "Why us?" they say. "We may be tasty, and there may be *many* recipes for us, but we feel there should be other birds (and why birds?) used for this great day. It is *not* a great day for us! We are cooked and stuffed, for heaven's sake!" Who came up with this idea? I heard some people today talking about the best way to cook a turkey. I bet if they were talking about the best way to stuff a dog (heaven forbid) or cat, there would be protesting for at least a year in form of riots, gunshots, and fires!

It is time to change this horrible tradition! I have been protesting for my friends for four days now. I have had *no* sleep, and guess what!

My own dad (after me yelling, screaming, and crying) sill cooked a turkey today! I am *not* speaking to him! Sorry, my turkey friends. I tried! I will protest this horrible tradition for the rest of my life. Such a thing would *never, ever* happen in Hungary!

Again, sorry! I will start protesting earlier next year. I will make sure that my dad does not order a turkey next year.

Love,

Veni

Letter 18

Dear Veni,

This is a tradition, for dog's sake! Most turkeys like to be in the middle of a beautiful table. Get over it!

Hoover

Letter 19

Merry Christmas to all my friends!

This is my third Christmas in the United States of America. My house is all decorated. The difference between this year and last is Mom insisted that Levi and I had to help decorate. Mom said we are a herding breed, and we need a job. Demi was not even asked! Mom gave her the day off because her job is to retrieve birds... not! I have never seen her even look at a bird! So as Levi and I helped Mom *all day long*, Demi was perched on the back of the couch in her regular spot. She is spoiled!

It was a very difficult job to carry the glass balls to the tree and even more difficult to keep myself from chewing on the wooden ornaments. (I have to admit that I hid one in the corner to eat later). Our house does look beautiful though. But the worst part is we have to take them all down when Christmas is over!

As you know, Mom has kept me very busy this year with herding (love it because I get to see Clint), agility, and obedience. Her plan for me in 2015 is a new thing called nose work, conformation classes, herding, and to take me to dog shows. She is afraid to enter me yet because of my personality glitch. I do not like strangers going over my body. Would you? Mom told me to get over it!

We will go (I am the only dog allowed) to my brother Chris's house for Christmas Eve, then my brother, Shawn's house for Christmas day. Mom is baking cookies for the kids, Nicholas, Ava, Avery, and Gage. And of course, we are *never* offered a cookie! After all that decorating, you would think that Mom would at least offer us one. We will work on Dad. He always gives in.

Merry Christmas and happy New Year to all. Demi, Levi, and I already have our hats and horns for New Year's Eve. Mom and Dad are going to allow us to have a sip of champagne at midnight. Just a sip they say!

I will send photos of the house in a couple of weeks.

Love,

Veni

PS: Mom and Dad say merry Christmas also!

Letter 20

Oh my gosh!

Mom and Dad's best friends who they shared New Year's Eve and New Year's with had a horrible experience right after New Year's Day. Jayleen was putting all her Christmas decorations away, and she slipped and fell down three steps. She shattered her femur bone (the biggest bone in her leg) and had to go to the hospital, had surgery, and got out three days later. She was in a lot of pain! After almost three weeks in a nursing home for therapy, she is finally getting out. She is going home but has to be extremely careful!

This is where I come in. First, she should have called me to help her with her Christmas decorations. I had lots of experience at my own home, as you might recall. I did not break *one* ornament! Mom has offered my services at her home. I am supposed to help cook, clean, and cook and clean! However, Jayleen does have two dogs of her own—a Scottie named McGiver and a cocker mix named Gracie. I really think that they should not be sitting on their rears while I do all the work. Do you? No. I am going to show them what to do, and I will expect them to help. Would you believe that they get their human mom up two times during the night to go out to potty? I *am going to put a stop to all this nonsense*! They are taking advantage of their mom and dad. They are going to learn to hold it, for heaven's sake!

I went to visit Jayleen in the nursing home. *Everyone* thought I was cute and talked about my great ears. One person even said I was beautiful. *Finally...* Ha, Demi! And guess what? I met the nicest lady from Hungary. She spoke half Hungarian and half English. I was the only one there that could understand her. It made me very homesick for my country, my brothers and sisters, and my human mom Kriztina. Miss you, Mom!

I am sending you a picture of my new friend.

Love,

Veni

PS: I will keep you informed about my job. Mom is making me study cookbooks. Demi is in charge of taking me to the grocery store. Thanks, Mom! This sounds like a lot of work!

Letter 21

Hi, Veni,

Happy New Year to you and your family. Please don't worry about not being asked to join in the Christmas festivities. My folks left me at the babysitter's for Christmas week. I didn't tell them, but I love my babysitter and all her other dogs. We sleep on her bed and also go in and out of the house anytime we wish. She is also a pushover for extra treats, etc.

New Year's was spent at home, and no matter how much I tried, my eyelids start drooping around seven thirty. Dad was happy to see this so he had a good excuse to go to bed early also. I know your evening lasted longer than that!

I hope you win lots of ribbons and medals in 2015. Your really are a beautiful girl.

Your investor,

Toby

Letter 22

Dear Toby,

Just wanted to tell you that I had the same problem on New Year's Eve. Mom and Dad went to bed early, and we three dogs joined them. Mom was not speaking to me because of the little incident at their friend's house. I snuggled up to her in bed nonetheless. She kept moving away, but I would move with her until she almost fell out of bed. She finally gave up. I smiled!

Love,

Veni

Letter 23

To all my dog friends,

It is my second Christmas in the United States. I mention that I had to help decorate the tree, make cookies, and help Mom make two salads. I also told you that I was the only dog invited to Christmas Eve at sister Susan's mother's house, and to my brother Shawn and sister Tori's house for Christmas day.

Long and sad story short, I did not get to go to either house. I spent both days and night in my crate at home with Levi and Demi—only Levi and Demi got to make themselves comfortable on Mom and Dad's bed! It was Mom's idea not to take me to sister Susan's mom and dad's house. It was raining, and she was afraid I would make a mess. This was okay because they were not gone long, and besides, I got to go the next day to brother Shawn's. *Not*! Mom called to tell brother Shawn that she was going to take a *big* plate of cookies. This is when Shawn said that they had decided that I should stay home because I *might* get into Avery's toys! With alligator tears in my eyes, I was asked to kennel up. I asked Mom if I could have a pen and paper to write. I had to get some things off my chest. I may not have a good reputation, *but* I have changed.

I spent many a day making food, feeding Avery and Gage in bed in the morning… Why does Avery not trust me? I love her so much! Well, this was my 2014 Christmas.

Letter 24

Hi, everyone,

I have not had a head cold in years. The one I was blessed with started after Christmas. It was a real doozy! I sneezed about every two minutes, blew my nose every four minutes, and looked much Rudolph! Rudolph should have been so lucky to have a nose as red as mine!

I had to go to the store to buy several rolls of toilet paper and Kleenex three times in two weeks. I am not quite sure what attracted Veni to my used Kleenex, but I would no sooner put it on my bathroom counter after use than it would be snatched up at the precise moment I put it down. It became a fight between Veni and me *every day*! If I was not fast enough, she would run into the other room, and sometimes offer to share with Levi. Levi, being the smart dog he is, told her that he was not interested.

She became faster and faster as the days of the cold of the century wore on. I did not feel well, so I was truly ready to shoot one little pumi! I thought about offering Veni a New York steak from one of the finest restaurants in Monterey County if she would just kindly give a one-minute break from the delicious Kleenex. She declined the offer—go figure!

I am praying not to have another cold for years to come!

Pam

Letter 25

Hi, Hoover,

I was at the barnyard in Carmel helping Mom train a Lab. I understand that she is related to you. She is cute, but not has handsome as you (even though you have a scar). I have changed my mind about scars. I think they are sexy. I just learned this word! Mom and Dad were watching a movie about a pirate. He had a scar and was very handsome (and sexy). Some pirates have a peg leg and an eyepatch also. My sister, Susan, told Mom (after Dad lost part of his leg) that she always knew Dad was a pirate. Mom laughed! I, on the other hand, did not think it was very funny!

While I was helping Mom train Sandy, the dog, a woman came out of a store (a beauty shop) and said to Mom that I was the "cutest" dog she has ever seen. (Never beautiful, just cute, ugh!) She wanted to know if she would take me to her shop after training. Mom did, and I met a lot of women! They all stared at me and sweet talked. "*Oh*! You are so adorable!" (Again, not beautiful!) They all talked about how cute my ears were. Why not my beautiful face! I wanted to ask the owner (who loved me) if I could get a beauty treatment.

They took a picture of me laying on Mom's jacket. I am going to ask Mom if I can go to her shop for a beauty treatment for my next birthday. Do not forget about diamonds, Hoover!

Love,

Veni

PS: I have been going for herding practice every Saturday. I *was* doing very well. I do a really fast down with a hand signal but have been getting a little lazy. Mom was really mad at me this week! She is going to torture me with practice. I can just feel it coming on. I have a hiding place!

Letter 26

Hi, Veni,

If it helps you feel better, I consider you one of the most beautiful girls I know. You're rather tall for me to get too interested in. However, your eyes (very sparkly), nose, and ears do combine to make you not only adorable, but very beautiful. Don't worry about the beauty treatments. You don't need them.

Fondly,

Toby

PS: Your stock portfolio has been doing very well. I will continue to manage it with a very watchful eye. Soon you'll be rich enough to buy your own diamonds!

Letter 27

Hi, Veni,

Thank you for calling me handsome. We could be the best-looking couple ever. I bet we would get offers for advertising and TV commercials. We could even get the next Super Bowl Budweiser commercial. We could star in the remake of the *Pirates of the Penzance*.

Love and kisses,

Hoover

Letter 28

Dear friends,

I am so busy with my presidential campaign, but Mom is training (I think he is training her) this handsome boy, Beau. I can't help myself. I stare at him outside the car window and feel myself falling in love. He has big eyes and big ears (like me). My mom kisses him all the time. I told her that is *my turn*!. I am getting a little jealous.

He asked to get on my dating service for dogs, but I want him myself. I do not know how to tell him. I would write to "Dear Veni," but this is me!

Any suggestions, my friends?

Love, and in love,

Veni

PS: He is a French bulldog. I am Hungarian. Do you think we would be a good match? And if marriage is in the future, should I get a prepup?

Letter 29

Dear Veni, *wow,* do *not* let this boy get away! I hope you are spayed though. I have found over the last four months where puppies come from. I also know that I cannot stand puppies! That being said, perhaps you might give Beau a gentle tug on his tail and then run the other way? Don't run too far. These Frenchies can't run too fast. Then play hard to get, but just for a few minutes! Hope this helps.

Your friend,

Willow

Letter 30

I am not spayed yet… long story! I will tell you about it sometime when there is more time, Willow. I thought you would agree, but I got a scathing e-mail from a white golden. He wants me too. He is angry that I picked Beau. Ahhh, what to do?

Love,

Veni

Veni For President

Hollywood

Letter 31

OMDog Hoover, Toby, Gunny, and Lexie,

I am so upset! Mom was asked to go to Hollywood to pitch *my* book for a movie, and did not invite me! I am the one that wrote the book! I am the one that writes to my auntie, my human mom, and all of you, not Mom!

She went without me. Boo-hoo! I could have pitched the book way better! She practiced in the car every day, several times a day. I was so sick of it! I will tell you what she said. "My dog Veni asked me to represent her today because she is so busy writing her second book." (*Not true*!. I did not ask her to represent me. I told her I wanted to go!)

Then she went on. "My book (not hers!), *Veni Vidi Vici,* is told by my dog Veni, who is a rare Hungarian herding breed born in Hungary. Veni learned when she was a little puppy that she was sold to some people from America. This made her very sad. She wanted to stay with her dog mom and her human mom and herd sheep in her native land." (This is true!)

"After she arrives in California from Italy, Veni gives us her perspective of other animals, humans, and her new mom, a dog trainer. Then she has to confront the challenge of being the new dog in the house. She meets Levi, another pumi, and Demi, a standard poodle who hates her from day one.

"Veni starts receiving letters from doggie pen pals with advice ranging from "stop your whining" to two Pomeranian brothers who offer to help her escape.

"There are so many twists and turns in Veni's life, such as almost going to Soledog prison to starting her own dating service for doggies. One never knows what her next story will bring, but one thing is certain. It *will* make you laugh!"

I am not laughing. I love my mom, but this was so unfair. Mom got to meet all the producers, went out to great dinners, and had fun with Aunt Leslie and my brother Chris. They also got to see some famous actors' homes. I want to star in my own movie and become famous like Lassie.

Mom found out yesterday that three producers want to read my book. They all have different ideas. Some want me to be a fake dog. I am going to put my paw down on this idea! It is *my* book and *my* decision. I will refuse to sign anything unless they let me star in my own movie!

I am calling my attorneys, Johnnie Collieran and Christopher Doxie, today!

Love,

Veni

Letter 32

Hi, Veni,

Hold off on calling those attorneys. You know your mom and dad are very poor. Your mom is even going to stand on street corner next week with a sign that says, "Need food, please buy my book." So you need to take anything these producers are willing to offer. The producer that was going to make you a fake dog just might make you a princess, and I could be your prince. Now I would consider buying you those diamonds that you have always wanted.

Love,

Hoover

Letter 33

Okay, okay, Hoover. Okay, okay, okay! Did you know that even though the three producers want to read the book, they still may not use it! Mom says it is an honor, but if they are smart (like me), they will let me do the movie. Hoover, you know I am cute (beautiful), right? Diamonds—*yes*!

Love,

Veni

Letter 34

Oh Veni,

I was wondering how you felt about your mom leaving you home while she got to go and talk about *your* book, not *hers*! I felt really sorry for you, but my mom said it's no place for Veni to be! Can you believe that? She agreed with your mom! That really made me mad. I almost refused to eat my dinner that night, I was so mad, but then my stomach started growling and I got hungry and ate my dinner as well as slowpoke Harley's, so I got in a lot of trouble!

I think we should plan a trip ourselves. Once they see you, they will fall so in love with you that they will not want a fake dog anymore, and your mom will have to take you with her next time she goes. We can stay at my sister Heather's house, where you can meet Sammy and Allie. They are the greatest dogs. You will love them. Just think, Veni. You are going to be so famous! Beautiful gowns, diamonds, cars, *men*! Yikes! I am so excited for you. Just remember, don't sign anything unless you have had your attorney read the fine print, even if they try to bribe you.

I am on my way home with my dad. I am so hungry, and he always puts a tiny bit of food in my plate. No wonder I eat Harley's food too. I am starving! You think your mom and dad have problems. My dad is really, really poor. Every time my mom says she wants a bigger house or something new, Dad rolls his eyes and shakes his head and says she should have married a rich man. I will not even tell you what Mom's response is! Well write me back, and don't worry, we will fix this.

Love you lots and lots,

Lexi

Letter 35

Dearest Veni,

Your quietness was overwhelming. I kept wondering when you would break your silence and let everyone know where you stood on this matter. It sounds like your mom is seeking fame at your expense. Keep this under wraps. Maybe confer with Hoover. He will give you the direction you need. I do think you need to be on your best behavior as the penal institutions love the young, naive ones. Be sure to have someone guard your backside, Veni.

Always,

Jude

Letter 36

Thanks, Auntie. Good thing I am *not* naïve, huh!

Veni

Letter 37

Dear Veni,

My mom forwarded your e-mail to me. I am in a town far away. Your mom was very unfair to you! I am glad that you are contacting your lawyers. Does your mom know about this? If so, I hope she does not "forget" to feed you!

Your friend,

Willow

Letter 38

To all my friends,

This is so embarrassing! From herding practice to a *tutu*! Ava did it. I could not say no because she is so cute. But I hated every minute of it!

Veni

Back to Reality

Letter 39

To all my friends!

I had the best day of my life yesterday! First and foremost, Mr. Clint *finally* got back from herding shows after a month! I could hardly wait to see him. He looked so good!

And then, a really wonderful thing happened on the same day. Mr. Clint told my mom that she is too strict with me. *Finally*! He told her that because she is a dog trainer, she expects too much from me. A little mini Aussie named Calle gave me a wink, and I smiled back. He lectured her for about an hour! He told her that she expects me to go down every time she tells me. Mom was not happy because she does expect me to do go down every time she tells me. Sometimes I *do not want to!*

Mr. Clint told Mom to tell me to *stop*. I do not understand what this means yet. And then, he keeps telling Mom to walk faster. She walks in front to the sheep. I heard her talking to herself on the way home. She said, "What does he expect! I have short legs. Does he want me to get roller skates?" Mr. Clint gave Mom a plastic water bottle with some rocks in it for me when I do not listen to her when she asks me to stay. She wants to use this on the sheep when they walk too fast, and maybe Mr. Clint too?

Love,

Veni

PS: Not to worry, Mr. Clint. I will not allow Mom to throw that water bottle at *you*!

Letter 40

To all my dog friends!

I met a *very* handsome dog that Mom is training. His name is Dodger, and he is from Belgium. He had to learn to speak English, just like me. I just *love* his accent! He told me that he thinks I am beautiful. Do you know how long I have wanted to hear *beautiful*? So many dogs tell me that I am a cutie, or I look just like a bear, a rabbit, or a Koala bear. They all love my ears. Dodger is the first dog that likes the whole package. He is a herding breed just like me! He promised to write. I am hoping to get flowers soon. I just have a feeling! Sigh!

If this relationship does not work out, he asked if he could be on my dating service. What do my girldogfriends think?

Love,

Veni

Letter 41

Hi, Veni. My name is Stella. My sister is Willow. She is traveling to shows and is not allowed to use Margie's laptop. Hope you do not mind if I chime in. Wait for flowers first from Dodger. When they arrive, thank him profusely and suggest he change his name to McCovey, Mays, or Buster. Let us know his response. If he asks about the dating service again, dump him!

Best from Stella

Letter 42

Dear Stella,

Thanks for your advice. Not to worry. If he prefers my dating service, I will sign him *after* I bite him on the leg! By the way, Stella, I know that you are a singer and have recently married. How is the doggie bar scene going, and your husband, Tank? Is Tank behaving himself? Do you see his brother, Coop? *And do* you suggest that I ask beautiful Demi to drive me over to the bar in Fresno? Perhaps I could meet some handsome boy dog?

Love,

Veni

PS: Could you please record my favorite love song so I can present it to my human boyfriend, Clint?

Letter 43

Hi, dog friends!

Tessie's dad bought one of my books, and guess who read it? When her mom and dad were at work, she decided to take a peek. She said that she liked my photo on the front, then found out that I herd sheep, so she decided to find out more about me. Mom trained Tessie and says that she is very smart! I am quite certain that she is not as smart as me, however!

But after reading about the chairs, bedspread, pillows, rugs, etc., that I chewed, a little mischievous thought crept into her brain. She decided that she should do something about it! When her dad arrived home, he found her at the door to greet him. (She read about me chewing a hole through the trunk of the car when I was stolen.) She chewed through her crate (it was upside down), chewed her mom's favorite chair, and peed on the rug.

Well, Tessie, I am so sorry that your dad got mad at you! It was not your fault. This just might teach him a lesson. (He has, after all, been training you!) You told me that you are lonely and would like a friend!. I just hope and pray you do not get one like Demi!

Love,

Veni

Letter 44

Pam,

That is it! I'm quitting my day job. Tess and I are buying a case of Pirate Beer, a van, and matching sunglasses and taking our routine on the road. Now if I can only get her to stop going on and on about Clint. "Clint this, Clint that, and did you see when Clint and I, etc." all the way back home. Oh brother was it nauseating (eye roll).

Tess appreciates her small but loyal fan base. As a token of her appreciation, she will be forwarding a few signed photos to you (at a nominal charge) sometime soon.

Sincerely,

The Management Team

Letter 45

Dear Mr. Freediver (and by the way, what does this mean?),

Would you kindly tell your dog, Tess, the perfect, that Clint is mine, and only mine! Oh yes, she did work for Clint, unlike me, who needed her Mom, but I *know* that Clint likes me and only me!

I will bring some Pirate beer to the next herding lesson. It will be for Tess, not you, Patrick! She will be too woozy to cuddle with Clint!

Love,

Veni

Letter 46

Hi, my friends. Guess what? Today is my third birthday! Am I getting old? I really do not want to look like Demi with all that gray on her muzzle! Ugh.

Love,

Veni

Letter 47

Veni,

Very good job. However, your mother has it all wrong. I was trained by her for months. I still remember, but she has forgotten. The sheep are supposed to be on her left side, not behind her.

Love,

Hoover

Letter 48

Happy birthday, Veni! No, you are not getting old. Just turned three myself.

Best from Stella.

Letter 49

To all my dear friends.

What a surprise… I am in trouble again! Mom and Dad invited their friends over for dinner with their dog Tessie. Tessie is a cow dog just like me. Of course, Demi was nice to her (why does Demi hate *me*?). They played and ran. I was stuck in the bedroom with Levi. Mom felt that we would not be nice to poor little Tessie, who is bigger than me, by the way! Levi was not allowed to meet her (he is obsessive about what he considers *his* property!). But Mom decided to test me (Tessie's dad was nervous and wanted to know if there was a veterinarian close by.) Mom took Demi back to the bedroom and let me out.

Tessie stared at me (she is only ten months old with tons of energy!), and I did not like it! She came over to me, and I nipped her. Mom was angry! She threw a dog collar at me. Not nice! Tessie, the cow dog, stayed clear of my territory the rest of the night. I hid behind Mom. Actually, she kind of frightened me. I do not like to admit this part of my personality. And, no, I refuse to take antidepressants! I would act just like Demi. I cannot think of anything worse.

Mom was so unhappy with me that I was not even offered our usual Sunday pancakes! This is the only day we are allowed people food. And guess what kind of pancakes I missed. Pumpkin! Demi and Levi expounded about how delicious they were. "Wow these are *soooo* good!" On and on and on. Demi was the loudest with her disgusting French accent!

I went to my bed for the rest of the day. Mom made me read books on dog behavior. Levi came to check on me and asked how I was doing. I could smell pumpkin pancakes on his breath. I told him to go away and leave me alone.

Depressed,

Veni

Letter 50

Dear Tessie,

This, I guess, is an apology letter. Mom said that my social skills are at a minus one, and that I, in no uncertain terms, must start working very hard to change my personality. She said, like was suggested at one time in my young life, that I am a candidate for shock treatments. She is calling the doggie psychiatrist first thing Monday morning.

I do want to be mean. It just creeps up on me. I did not know you, Tessie! You are black and white for one, and you kept staring at me! I felt like I had to let you know that this was my house, and you must behave. Mom just told me that this is no excuse. She tells me that I am not to make those kinds of decisions. Well, I am sorry I guess. I do not know how to change yet, but will be going to the doctor tomorrow. FYI, I am afraid of all the dogs at class. You will see Monday night. I bark first though.

Veni Jackson

PS. From Demi Jackson. I told *everyone* that Veni is a brat. Now you know the truth. I am the best dog in the Jackson family!

Letter 51

Dear Veni,

I just hate rainy days. It is so difficult to find a place to go potty without getting your paws dirty. We have a big oak tree in the yard that I climb to look out at the world sometimes, and it occurred to me this would be a great place to go potty. It was a little difficult to maneuver, but it works! What do you think? I just might be onto something. Maybe you could share this knowledge with some of your friends.

Your friend,

Stanley

Footnote

Dear friends, look at this!

Hoover and his mom enjoying a martini. You notice I am a just a beer drinker! I think he could afford diamonds, don't you?

Love,

Veni

Maybe we could put the two photos together?

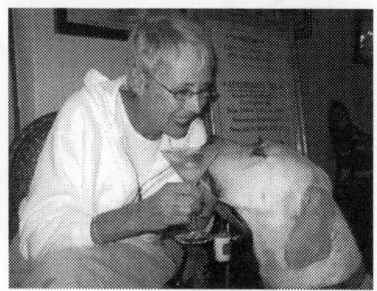

Letter 52

To my dear doggie friends.

It is Thanksgiving time again! You know how I feel about those poor turkeys. I am giving all my doggie friends fair warning to get outside and talk to all your turkey friends and suggest that they *get out of town fast!* Mom gives me a small amount of money to do my chores (babysitting, cleaning Levi's eyes, cleaning up the toilet paper that has been spreading around the bedroom), and guess who is guilty? *Demi, yes, perfect, Demi*! I suggest that we pool our money and get those poor turkeys airline tickets to Europe. Not Paris though! Did you know that Europeans do not celebrate Thanksgiving? I am positive that you are aware of this, but I just wanted to make sure. We do not have too much time, so gather up your money so we can help them! Let's get together for a meeting ASAP. Ask your Mom and Dad for a little extra money!

Mom and Dad are leaving us for nine days. I heard them talking about taking me with them, but Mom is thinking it may be more of a vacation for her if I stay home. After all I do for her! I do obedience (and I might add, I do a very good job!), I herd sheep for her, etc. My feelings are hurt! If they decide *not* to take me, at least I will not have to see one of those poor, poor cooked turkeys.

Suggestion—act sick and throw up (a little diarrhea might help too) if you see a turkey at your house!

Love,

Veni

Letter 53

Dear doggie friends,

I cried and cried—and they gave in!

I went on a nine-day vacation in Oregon with Mom and Dad! Levi and Demi had to stay home because they did not have room in the car. Yes. It was all about *me*! I did feel sorry for Levi, however! But Mom and Dad sprang for the best dog sitter in Monterey County. Her name is Amanda. They thought about leaving them by themselves (you know how poor they are), but Mom saved some money from my book sales. Where is my percentage?

First of all, I am going to tell you about every day of my nine-day trip because it was very interesting, but first of all I have to write an apology to Aunt Leslie! It was very cold at the Oregon coast, so Mom, Dad, Aunt Leslie, and Uncle Mike left me in the car while they enjoyed a wonderful dinner. This, in fact, was far from fair. Do you think? Same old story, they eat a special dinner, and I get nothing. Dessert might have been nice!

Mom got in the car first because she was driving. Dad got in the front seat, and then Aunt Leslie opened the door to get in the backseat. I took one look at her and bolted! (You might remember that I thought she was a ghost when she stayed at our house. Come on! White nightgown and white hair!) I know she is a ghost, so I ran. Aunt Leslie saved my life (almost lost hers) because she stopped all the cars as I ran across the street. After Mom saw what happened, she jumped out of the car (I was across the street in a grassy area). Mom ran over, put her arm up, and said *down*. I hit the ground! (Take note, Clint!) She told me to stay, then carried me back to the car. Everyone in the car was *very* upset, especially Aunt Leslie, who almost met her demise running in front of a car. Auntie was not only very angry at me but was not at all happy with Mom! She told Mom that she felt I was more important than her!

Not true, Auntie. Mom loves you! She is sorry, and so am I, but I have to tell the truth. I still think you are a ghost!

Love,

Veni

PS. A little dessert might have helped avoid the whole fiasco. Huh!

Footnote: Yikes, poor Veni! I would have run too. I am afraid of ghosts. Congratulations on doing an excellent down stay. You should have been given at least a bite of dessert for crying out loud!

Your friend,

Willow

Letter 54

Hi, all,

We left about 11:00 a.m. on the Thursday before Thanksgiving for our nine-day vacation. Mom drove us to a place called Mt. Shasta, California. We had reservations in Redding, but Mom knew how much Dad loves Mt. Shasta, so Dad told a little white lie (not good) and canceled our reservations in Redding. (I was always told *not* to tell a lie!) I did mention this to Dad!

We arrived at Mt. Shasta just as it was getting dark. Dad told me a bedtime story even before it was bedtime. We were still in the car. He told me that Mt. Shasta is a very spiritual place because little people live around the mountain and they are called Lumerians. They are a very old race. There have been many spaceships spotted around the mountain at various times also. In the town, there are many paintings of spaceships, and some of the townsfolk have seen the Lumerians. Now, would you like to stay in a town like this? I was so frightened that when I went out to go potty, I did it *really* fast.

Mom and Dad were allowed to take me into the restaurant for dinner. I was such a good girl. I stuck right by Mom. Of course, everyone wanted to see me. "Oh, what cute ears she has," they all said. There were a few short people in there. I am sure they were Lumerians! My little ears were shaking. Right after dinner, we settled in our room. Mom and Dad went to sleep, but I slept with one eye open because I could hear those little Lumerians talking. They were close to our motel looking for food. This was the worst night of our trip! I was so tired. I slept all the way to Eugene, Oregon, the next day. Whew. I was so glad to leave Mt. Shasta. I never want to hear of a Lumerian again!

Love,

Veni

PS: I did not see any spaceships around the mountain, thank dog! Oops, I mean God!

Letter 55

To all my friends,

We arrived in Eugene, Oregon, about five on Friday night. There were so many suitcases, hanging clothes, and my food (most important) that it seemed it took about an hour to unload the car when we arrived at Aunt Leslie's house. Uncle Mike helped with everything with Mom's help also. Dad still cannot do much with a walker and his new prosthesis.

The house was very scary because it was soon filled with lots and lots of people and grandkids, all running and screaming. Between Aunt Leslie and Uncle Mike, there had to be a least a hundred kids! The Lumerians were looking better and better! I stayed right at Mom's feet—the safest place. I have to admit, though, that I loved their backyard. I saw an animal in the backyard with a long, bushy tail. Mom told me that it was a squirrel. I chased it, but could not catch it. I ran really fast! Then I chased birds. Every place I looked there was something to chase.

Then back into the house with hundreds of people. I pleaded with Mom to please leave me in the backyard. She told me no because I would jump the fence and try to run home. Good idea!

It was soon time to go to bed. Thank God! Dad is still not comfortable in bed, so he slept in their recliner in another room. It was very peaceful in bed with Mom. The kids were gone, and the Lumerians were in Mt. Shasta, so I slept well.

On the morning of day 3, Mom took me out to go potty. It was cold, but I loved it! I went back in the house to eat breakfast. Uncle Mike kept calling me over to see him. I almost went, but after all, he is married to the ghost! I finally went over to see him. He is very nice because he talked to me all the time. I could tell that he was sad about something. Then I heard them talk about just losing their dog, Carlie. He cried. I felt very sorry for him! Even though Carlie was a standard poodle, I still felt sorry for Uncle Mike!

Soon, there were the same one hundred people and kids over for the Oregon football game. Again, yelling and screaming! My little ears will *never* be the same! I do like kids, I have to admit, but there are quite a few tall men in their family. They frightened me. They could stomp on me with one foot, and I would be a pancake!

We headed to bed after everyone left, and again, I enjoyed my time with Mom, but in the morning, just as soon as she opened the door, I ran into Dad's room and jumped on his chair with him—tail wagging and kisses galore! I even jumped on Uncle Mike's bed. This may be the time that he started really liking me?

On day 4, we packed up and left for the Oregon coast. I will relate all later!

Love,

Veni

Letter 56

Dear Hoover,

I wanted to tell you more about my trip to Oregon. When we left Eugene (just Mom, Dad, Aunt Leslie and Uncle Mike), we stopped at a coastal town named Yachat. We did a little shopping (Mom's favorite thing; Dad is not as impressed!), then had lunch (of course I was not invited even though I am a service dog for Dad), more shopping, then time for dinner. Gee, I was so lucky. I got my dinner first. Nice of them to finally think about me!

The next day, we left for New Port. We stayed right by the sea. Mom walked me outside our room to the potty area. I got to meet many dogs and watched them walk by our room. I jumped on the couch so they all thought I was a big dog. I told them that I was a Rottweiler! This made them walk faster. I was even allowed to go out off-leash. I stayed right by Mom, looking right and left. One cannot be too careful!

We stayed in New Port for two days. Mom and Aunt Leslie found a great shop (of course), and Mom told the owner about me. She told her that I wrote a book (nice of her to *finally* admit it!). Mom had my book in her purse, so the owner wanted to see it, started reading, and then laughed. She bought the book. Mom and Aunt Leslie found many shops, despite the bored looks on Dad and Uncle Mike's face.

The second night was the night that Aunt Leslie and I almost died. I wrote about this already, and really do not want to talk about it again—too traumatic!

We were gone for three days, then went back to Eugene for Thanksgiving. I refused to look at the turkey! There were thirty people at my cousin's (Scott and Donna) home. It was *very* stressful, so I had a little problem. I had to use the grass many, many times that day and night. I was sick. I feel so sorry for those poor turkeys. I know that this was my problem!

We left for Medford, Oregon, to see more relatives the day after Thanksgiving. We really had a good time with Aunt Millie, cousin Judy, and TZ. We stayed at cousin TZ's house that night. At 3:00 a.m., I whined at our door. Mom got up to take me outside. She bumped into walls and almost tripped in the dark, but we made it. It was very cold, but Mom stayed out with me, telling me to *hurry up*! It did take a while. Cousin TZ's husband, John, said that he would think about Veni and me when he slipped and slid, picking up leaves in his backyard. I am not quite sure what he was talking about?

The following day, we drove home. I was so happy! I missed Levi. When we made our turn by our house, I started barking and whining. Mom and Dad looked at each other. They both mentioned that they did *not* miss my barking. Yes, I had a vacation all by myself, and I know

I should be thankful… *but* please take Levi next time! If a wild dog tried to attack me, he would take care of business. Okay, okay. I am the toughest dog in the family, but a little reinforcement always helps!

Love,

Veni

Hoover, Mom has promised bedtime stories. I asked to hear about all the dogs she adopted from the time she was a little girl. I can tell you that she told us about her very first dog that she named Taffy. She was a cocker spaniel. Mom saw her at a pet shop in Klamath Falls, Oregon, and threw a fit until her mom bought her! Mom told me that most pet shops are bad. They did not give poor Taffy any vaccines, so she only lived two weeks. Very sad story. Mom cried and cried until her second dog appeared in her life. This is a happier story. Tell you later!

Letter 57

Hi, Veni,

Yes, Veni, I have discovered a new best friend. My dad feeds me twice a day. He plays ball with me every day. He plays frisbee with me every day. He gives me a cookie every night. He walks me when it's not too hot or cold. We were at our cabin in Lake Tahoe for the New Year. My dad still played ball with me on the beach covered with snow. The temperature was eighteen. But my mom has become my new best friend. She spends hours in the kitchen, and I am always by her feet. When she sits, I will put my head in her lap as long as she will let me. I think I am going through a middle age crisis. I will be turning forty-two this month.

Veni, I think we should continue to be friends and keep in contact, but I am getting too old for you and don't have the energy I used to have.

Your friend,

Hoover

Letter 58

This makes me very sad, Hoover! Perhaps you need some professional help? I am twenty-one, which makes me old enough to go to dog bars now. Are you certain that you are too old for me? I disagree. I like older boy dogs. Perhaps we could meet for a drink at the famous dog bar, Drinks for Doggies, in Monterey for a little talk. Your mom is your mom, not your girlfriend, for heaven's sake, Hoover. What are you thinking?

Love,

Veni

Letter 59

My dear Hoover,

I am just now learning at this very moment that we passed your home! OM gosh, I could have been whining, howling, and crying if I would have known. I do remember seeing a sign for Sacramento. Mom and Dad were so uptight (happens a lot) about leaving late, that even if I would have fainted on the way, they would have continued driving. They are driven!

Perhaps you can send me a train ticket? Or should I be heading to Denver? Your cousin did offer pasta, wine, chocolate, and a diamond!

Let me know the plan.

Lots of love,

Veni

Letter 60

Veni,

Do you mean to tell me you drove right by my house and you did not stop to see me? I came to your book signing just to see you, and all I got was a down stay from your mom. I would have even let you stay at my house, and your parents could have picked you up on their way home. We don't have Lumerians in Sacramento. You would have been safe.

If you are still on the road, you better stop and see me on your way home or I just might need to look for another girlfriend.

Love,

Hoover

Letter 61

To all my doggie friends,

My mom has had a very bad week! She says that she does not like fleas or birds. I told her that this is not nice. They are both God's creatures and should be loved. She told me that she does not like fleas!. Somehow our house was inundated with fleas. We doggies had our medication to rid them, but for some reason, Mom and Dad (and they do not even like him. desperate!) had many flea bites. Mom spent the whole day vacuuming all the rugs in our house so the pest control could come to kill them. I feel a little bad about this, but I have to admit that I do not like fleas either! Levi is very allergic to them—poor guy. Mom has flea bites all over her body, including her head. I have to say, you fleas have to think about someone other than yourselves! You make life very difficult to those who do not appreciate your intrusion. Think about it! You could ask for an invitation!

Now about the birds! Not only did Mom spend the day vacuuming, but she had to clean all the bird poop piled a mile high on the back porch, the front of the garage, and the front of the house. Company is coming! *Swallows*. She spent worked for three hours just on bird poop.

Fleas and birds! Come on, Mom. At least you did not have to do Julian Michaels! Think about it—you did not have to do your exercise videos today. Don't worry, be happy.

Love you, Mom,

Veni

Letter 62

Bedtime story for Demi, Levi, and Veni, requested by Veni. Veni wants to hear about all the dogs that Dad and I had over the years.

This story will be about some of our old English sheepdogs. Our very first sheepdog came from a pet store. This is a no-no, doggies! They come from puppy mills, where they just breed to make money. Her name was Lu Lu, and that she was! She was hyper and hated other dogs. She was not an easy dog to live with. Not saying that you dogs are perfect! I did show her in obedience and got a companion dog degree on her. I was one of the original members of Dog Training Club of Salinas Valley. Lu Lu never, *ever* rested in the car on the way to a show and on the way home. She had too much energy! The club gave me a surprise party after she got her degree because she was one of the toughest dogs to ever get a degree in the club!

When I was showing Lu Lu in obedience, I met a lady that was showing an OES in obedience also. However, her dog was showing in utility. This is the most difficult of all the degrees! She was a beautiful working dog. I talked to this lady, who mentioned that she was going breed this dog! Wow! I wanted one!

Shortly thereafter, Effie Belamey entered our lives. Be careful what you wish for, doggies! Effie came from a very smart mom.

Our very first episode happened when she was a little puppy. We lived in a two-story house in South Salinas at the time. I went upstairs to get dressed, and as I approached the bottom of the stairs, there was Effie in the living room covered with flour. She was pure white! Not only did she get the flour out of the cupboard, but the nuts also. Effie was making a cake! This was the start of much more to come. She learned how to open the bread drawer and the refrigerator. We had no idea why the refrigerator was open sometimes until she was brazen enough to open it right in front of us with her paw. We caught her walking by the fridge and sniffing. If there was nothing interesting, she would not bother to open it, but if there was something enticing (like meat), it was down her throat in seconds!

Then there was the time that we had a flag football party at our house with lots of people. One of mothers brought a beautiful cake with whipped cream on top. Effie was outside in her dog run, which connected to the garage. I went out to take the cake into the house when I discovered that the refrigerator door was open, and the whipped cream had some tongue marks on top. Oh *no*! I had to think fast. I went back into the kitchen, got a knife, and spread the whipped cream around the top (not much left), took it in, and served it! To this day, I have *never* told anyone about this!

And then there was the Harley story. Harley was painting the outside of our house. I thought it was safe to let Effie out for a while, while I took a bath. *Until* there was some frantic knocking on the back door. I threw on my robe, and ran downstairs. I opened the door, and in comes Effie with paint on her feet, which she got all over the kitchen floor. Harley's face was bright red (he was a little crotchety to begin with), and he said, "This dog just dumped over a thirty-gallon can of paint. Now you are going to have to pay for this!" As I cleaned up the kitchen floor, I called Dad to tell him to remember that there is humor in everything.

I went back upstairs, finished my bath, then went to the window (he was painting the upstairs) and told him that I was sorry. He said, "That's okay, but that damn dog (his words) climbed my ladder (it was a two-story ladder!), opened up my lunch pail, and ate my sandwich!" *Oh my gosh! Leave it to Effie,* I was thinking. I made another call to Dad to ask him to pick up a sandwich for Harley on his way home for lunch.

There are many more Effie stories to tell, but it is bedtime, doggies. I will tell you more tomorrow night. And Veni, I sometimes think that you are a reincarnation of Effie!

Mom

Letter 63

The Effie stories continue.

I trained Effie to compete in obedience. As soon as she was old enough, I started entering her in shows. I never knew what she was going to do in the ring because, just in case you did not know doggies, handlers are not allowed to correct their dogs when they are showing. If you have a smart dog (like Effie), they know this! And did she ever!

We sailed through novice obedience with flying colors. She got some good scores. A passing score is 170, and the highest score one can get is 200. To get a novice, open, and utility degree, you have to get three passing scores, also known as three legs. All her scores were in the 190s.

This is the easiest degree because your dog is only off leash a few times. It is a different story in open obedience, the next phase. There was only one caveat that I forgot to mention. I took your brother Chris to Bakersfield to a dog show with me. As we were all lined up for the sits and downs (the dogs are right in a row for a one-minute sit stay and a three-minute down stay). Chris had just bought a hot dog and was on his way back to the ring. I could see Effie's eyes looking at him, and her neck was rigid. She was staring at Chris's hot dog. I looked over and gave Chris a look to kill, which made him stop in his tracks until the stays were over. I took Effie out of the ring, and she pulled me to Chris and grabbed a bite of his hot dog. (There is *another* hot dog story to come!)

Open obedience is where Mom had to hide her head in shame as she left the ring. Many people gathered around the ring to watch what Effie might do next. I took her to a fun match the first time in open. These matches are where you are allowed to correct your dog if there is a problem. In open, your dog has to jump a high jump and a long jump and do a drop on the recall (call your dog, then ask them to go down in the middle, and then call them to you). It is all off-leash healing.

Effie scored a minus zero score at her first fun match. The reason that she had a minus is because, not only did she do *everything* wrong, but after she jumped the high jump, it took her *forever* to come back over the jump to me. Why? She pooped on the other side of the jump! I was mortified!

After a few more fun matches, I felt that she might be ready to show at a real show. Remember, she could not be corrected! There are two things that happened in open obedience that were very bad. She almost killed a judge! I threw the dumbbell over the high jump (she had to jump the maximum height), but I did not throw it far enough, so the judge had to go over to get it for me to throw it again. He was an old judge, so it took him awhile to get there. Just as he was leaning down to pick up the dumbbell, Effie started to take off. She was going to jump that high jump, and she would have landed right on the judge. I had to grab her. The judge did not see me, thank goodness, because, if he had, I would have been zeroed. I ended up getting a leg in open that day and saved a judge's life!

When we lived in South Salinas, I would go outside to practice with Effie. There was a Welsh corgi that lived down the street from our house. He belonged to a judge. The judge was always trimming his hedges, and when he turned his back, his little beloved corgi would run down the sidewalk and bite Effie on the rear. I would never allow her to retaliate. This happened many times.

When I was showing Effie in open obedience one day, I called her to me for the drop on the recall at the same time that a corgi was going for glove number one in utility. (I will explain utility later.) There was only a tape around the ring ropes. I saw the gleam in Effie's eyes! In a voice that told her she had better listen, I told her to go down. She did, but she still had her eyes on the corgi. Then I called her in. While she was still eyeing the corgi, she sat in front of me. Then I asked her to heel (which means to go to heel position). She did a beautiful jump finish, sat, then ran under the ring rope and jumped the corgi. It was like watching a cartoon where they go around and around in circles! Then she came back with a very pleased look on her face. She finally got her corgi! And doggies, you will never guess what happened!. My judge blamed the other judge for sending the corgi at the same time. I got another leg in open with a good score. And guess what else? The lady who owned the corgi was looking for me. She was *very* angry!

Effie got her open degree with scores in the 190s again. Then on to utility.

Bedtime, doggies!

Mom

Letter 64

The Continuing Effie Stories

Effie got her open degree with a few mishaps but nonetheless, pretty darn good scores! Now on to the most difficult degree in obedience: utility. Utility is mostly off leash, with hand signals for the jumps. A dog has to go over a bar jump and a high jump and has to be sent out for this with a command. *Go*! One of the most difficult exercises in utility are the scent articles. One set is leather and the other aluminum. I had to turn Effie away from the articles, scent them up with my hands, leather first, then aluminum, ask her to heel to face the articles, then send her out to find the one that had my scent. Not easy! Utility ends with a stand stay where your dog is lined up with all the dogs competing. Many dogs move, sit, or lie down on the stay. If your dog messes up on any of these exercises, he or she fails.

Believe it or not, Effie never failed the scent articles, but there were many more ways to fail in Utility! First of all, Effie only got one leg in utility in a year of showing. This was not good, to say the least! She would mess up one thing each time I showed her. I needed two more to get her degree, but I finally gave up. Not easy for me to admit! The one time she qualified, she had a runoff for first place (same score) with another unusual breed, an Afghan. Effie came in second.

There were three comical things that Effie did in utility. I sent her out for the jumps. A handler wants the dog to go straight so he or she will be lined up perfectly for the hand signal to take one of the jumps. Effie went out so fast and straight that she hit the stake right in the middle (great go out!), but hit it so hard that she did a double back flip and landed perfectly straight!

Then after I sent her out for the jumps, I gave her a hand signal for the bar jump. She jumped it, but as she was coming in to me, she went to the judge first, jumped up, put her paws on his shoulders, and gave him a long kiss. She then came to me and did a beautiful straight sit in front of me. The judge was not sure how to score her on this!

Now for the famous Effie story. Hold on to your hats, doggies. This will make you laugh! As I was doing my off leash heeling with Effie this particular day, we had a judge who was running all of us up against the ring ropes on the turns. As I made a right turn, I felt that I lost Effie just a bit. She was always healing right on my left side, but I felt a brief loss. When I glanced down as we were still healing, I noticed that she was munching on something. She had *mustard* on her muzzle! As I looked back, I saw a little boy holding his hot dog with a confused look on his face. Effie had stolen part of his hot dog!

People could sit right next to the ring to watch the dogs performing in obedience. I would bet that this little boy never got close by a ring rope again. Ya think! And this judge did not know how to score her—give her points, or take them away.

Bedtime, but I will tell you that our two sheepdogs, Effie, and Mollie were both in the top ten highest scoring sheepdogs in the nation.

Nighty night, doggies!

Love,

Mom

Footnote: We had several sheepdogs in our lifetime: Effie, Mollie, Sophie, Lizzie, Chauser, Johnathan, and Reggie. I will tell a story about Reggie tomorrow night!

Champion Windfiled Sophie's Choice

Letter 65

Okay, doggies. It is time for another bedtime story. I promised I would tell you about our old English sheepdog, Reggie. Reggie was one of Sophie's puppies.

Reggie was a little grumpy, but there was a reason! He ate pyracantha berries every day. These are little red berries that the birds eat also. It makes them drunk. Well, guess what? Reggie was drunk *every day*! And when he came down, he was a total grouch! He did think about opening a business to sell them to all his doggie friends but decided to keep them all to himself.

When we moved to our home in Chualar Canyon, we were nervous about Reggie. How was he going to survive without his berries? We could not believe our luck! There were pyracantha berries in his new backyard. Whew! Problem solved!

Before you go running out in the backyard to look for the bush, I am thrilled to say it has been removed.

Good night, doggies. It is late!

Love you.

Letter 66

Good evening, doggies,

We also had two corgis, Bernie and Cedric. They were both adorable and herding breeds like you, Levi and Veni. I was asked by Hartnell College to train the dog for *Travels with Charley*, which was a standard poodle. We got Charley when he was a puppy. Cedric hated the competition of another male dog, so he disliked Charley from day one. We had to find the perfect home for Cedric, and did! One of my students had just lost her corgi, so she wanted Cedric. He went to her home and loved it. It was a difficult decision, but I felt that Cedric could handle a new home better than Charley.

Nighty night! I hope all you doggies get along. Just a thought!

Love,

Mom

Letter 67

Good evening, doggies,

And then there was Charley—a *very* special dog! As I mentioned, Charley came to us when he was nine weeks old. He was to be the star of the play John Steinbeck's *Travels with Charley*. I might add that I was asked to train the dog for this play because I had already trained two different dogs for the play *Annie*. Dad thought that we should get a standard poodle to train instead of looking for one that someone had in their family. When Charley arrived at the airport, it was love at first sight!

Charley started his training right away. He had to star in the play at fifteen months of age, which is very young. He was extremely smart, so he learned quickly, but there was a little problem. He worked well for me but would have to be trained by the star who played John Steinbeck. George Woods came into Charley's life several weeks before the play. George was a wonderful equity actor from Los Angeles.

Mom had to train George to train Charley. It was a must that Charley have respect for him. Mom did all the training from the side of the stage. Charley opened the play by going out to George with a collar in his mouth to start his traveling. The producer told all the actors that they were *not* to talk to Charley because Charley was an actor also.

Charley really wanted to be with me at first and ran off the stage when I gave him a signal. However, the producer wanted him to slow down. I had *no idea* how to slow him down! *But* as the weeks went on, Charley started sauntering off the stage. He liked his new profession! He became an actor.

One very embarrassing thing happened on stage. John Steinbeck traveled with Charley through the South. He came across a Southern bigot. He was a young actor who eventually went to New York to pursue his career. Charley was supposed to bark at him when he approached George. This young actor was so good that Charley was really ready to attack. George had to hold him back! This young actor played several parts in the play. Charley was on stage at the beginning of the play one night when I heard him barking. I was thinking, *Oh no*! I peeked though and saw Charley barking at the Southern bigot playing another part! *Ugh*!

Charley had seven plays and was on stage three-quarters of the time. He got wonderful reviews, but his favorite part was greeting all the people after each play was over. He pranced out wearing his ascot, waiting for all the compliments. He got what he wanted!

Now on to his show career!

It is late. I will finish up tomorrow night.

Nighty night, doggies!

Letter 68

Now on to Charley's show career! I had to grow out his coat to get him ready for the show ring. I found a handler to show him in Fresno. Her name was Margie.

She and her husband wanted us to drop Charley off at one of the shows. We met them there, and they took him home to start his show career. Margie's husband, Tim, made the mistake of telling us that Charley sat in the exercise pen *waiting* for us to come back. Margie was very mad a Tim for telling us.

Charley got used to the show ring like he did acting and finished his championship fairly quickly. Did I mention that Charley not only knew hand signals from the play but also did trick training? Margie and Tim could not figure out why Charley barked when they moved their hands a certain way! Tim finally figured it out, and they all laughed. I did notice that Tim always had a smile on his face when Charley's name was mentioned. He was one heck of a funny dog!

Did I ever tell you doggies that Charley saved my life one day when I was training? Yes. This actually happened. I was training in Prunedale out in the country. I had some time before my next student, so I took Charley for a walk on a desolate road. A tall man approached us coming from the opposite direction. He looked menacing, and he was. He came toward me, saying, "*Hey*!" Charley hit the end of his leash, barking and growling. The man backed up, saying, "Okay, okay!" I met a young woman on the same road pushing a baby stroller. I told her what happened, and she said that I was lucky to have a dog with me. He was her neighbor and was very scary.

I do not know if you understand this, Demi, Levi, and Veni, but a person can have a soul mate dog. Charley was one of those. He went to doggie heaven when he was eleven years old, and I miss him every day. His collar, as you all know, is right next to me in the car every day and always will be. All of you, and all the rest our doggies, are so very special also. And you are all one of a kind—especially you, Veni!

Footnote: Charley was our first standard poodle, but there were several others: Romeo, Garbo, Natalie, and Demi. Romeo, Garbo, and Demi all finished their championships also. I know that Demi likes to flaunt it, huh, Veni!

Love,

Mom

This is the end of the doggie stories, dogs. I need a little break. Dad has offered to take over.

Letter 69

Bedtime Story from Dad

Good evening, doggies,

Mom forgot to tell you about one of the most important animals in our household—*Spike*, our Maine coon cat! We had Spike for about fourteen years. He was one of the *greatest* cats ever! He was big and beautiful and loved all the dogs, and the dogs loved him.

There was only one time in his life that a dog went after him. It was when Bernie, our corgi, when she had her one puppy, Cedric. Spike was helping Bernie with her whelping. He was on top of her crate cheering her on when the puppy was born. He jumped off the top of her crate to leave the room for a few minutes. When Spike returned to check on her, Bernie ran after him, barking and growling. She would not allow Spike in the whelping area *again*! He was confused and devastated. After all, he did help her in her time of need. The look on his face said it all: *women*!

Time to hit the sack, doggies!

PS: There was another cat in our life also. He was a pixie bob, and his name was Sly. To be completely honest, he was one mean cat! He did not like the dogs, and the feeling was mutual. He would attack them for no reason. They were glad when he was gone!

Letter 70

Dear doggies, time for one last bedtime story,

How could I forget our llamas and alpacas! At one time, we had thirty-five of them. They are wonderful animals. They hum and only spit if they are hurt. Llamas are much larger than alpacas. Alpaca wool is very soft, and used in many types of clothing. Llamas are also used for backpacking, but many breeders use them for show, and alpacas also.

Mom wanted to show the alpacas, of course. It is in my blood! One time we went to Estes Park, Colorado, for a show. There were three of us that shared the driving, pulling a large horse trailer. We went over a high mountain close to Estes Park, and the transmission on my car went out. The pickup and trailer were on a major slope, so if the brakes failed, our alpacas would be heading down the hill. It was terribly frightening! A man drove by and offered to take our young man into town to get help. We let him go but thought perhaps we had made a mistake.

He made it back with a huge truck to take our pickup and trailer down the hill. Our alpacas stayed at an alpaca farm close by. They were enclosed in a secure barn so the bears could not get them. It was the trip from hell!

We had the llamas and alpacas for about five years, then sold them when your dad had to have heart surgery. We still have the barn, which makes me think about them every day. Wonderful animals!

Bedtime!

PS: We had a llama named Julio. He visited many nursing homes.

Letter 71

Dear Miss Suzi,

Thank you so much for teaching me how to use my nose! I can find *everything* now—on high counters, inside boxes, Mom's desk, the dining room table, the bathroom counter, the garbage that sits on *top* of the toilet (so I cannot get into it... *not*). Just today, I jumped on Mom's bathroom counter and finished off her yogurt while she was on the phone. She had to put a friend on hold because she heard the spoon hit the floor. Right after, I took one of her ink pens off her desk and jumped on her bed to eat it, but I got caught. I tried to be very quiet!

I check out *everything* in our home now. I push things with my nose, books, papers, face creams on Mom's counter, everything on Dad's counter. It is a mess, so it is much fun!

One can never be too careful!. I look for bombs in our house, the garage, and in all of the bushes outside. The FBI needs me. I am going to write them a letter asap. Navy Seal is still an option.

Thank you again, Miss Suzi. I would love to take another class, even though I am become somewhat of an expert.

Veni

My Run for President!

Letter 72

To all my friends,

After talking it over with all my family—my mom, my dad, my brothers and sisters, Levi, and even Demi (who just smirked... I should not have said a word to her!)—I am making a huge commitment. *I am running for president of the United States of America.*

I may not be a billionaire with a reality show, but I am famous too. I am a writer! And I know a lot about politics. After all, I listen to Mom's radio in the car and the news is on the TV at home all day. I speak three languages, so I know that I would do well with all the foreign dignitaries. I already have bodyguards, thanks to my Pomeranian friends, Chesty and Gunny. They are marines!

I am going to run as an independent (a natural for me). I know that I have missed Iowa and New Hampshire, but I can still I win. I am very intelligent and beautiful. I graduated high school with excellent grades and Cornell doggie college on the dean's list. When I decided that I wanted to be a lawyer, I was accepted to Harvard. (I needed a law degree to go after my dad's Dr. Z, as you might recall, the leg and arm thief.) I graduated in the top ten of my class. Those doggone border collies! They always are in the top ten also.

I know for sure that I can make this country good again! I do need your votes and some volunteers. I would like all breeds from the working and herding groups, and some Chihuahuas for my Hispanic friends. You have to promise to be nice when knocking on doors. Lifting your leg, growling, or smelling crotches will be *off limits*!

I do need help, my friends. Please let me know when you can go to work for me. You can vote *now* if you wish. Please send your vote via e-mail.

Thank you for all your help! *Veni for president!* Woo-hoo!

Veni

Letter 73

Hi Veni,

I would vote for you over any of the other candidates, but you have a problem. You were not born in the United States. Your real parents were not born in the United States. Now for a potential *bigger* problem. If Donald Trump becomes our next president, he is going to deport you. You better hide.

Love,

Hoover

Letter 74

Dear Hoover,

Don't you know that the rules *do not* apply to canines, you ninny! I was born in another country but was adopted by citizens of the United States. I have the papers to prove it. However, it does not really matter.

Donald Trump will not try to deport me because number one, I am going to beat him, and if he picks on me, I will send all my shepherd and rottweiler friends over to pay him a little visit at Trump Towers. I know how to play the game, Hoover.

Letter 75

Dear Veni:

You can count us in for your vote on the big election day. We think you would be a perfect fit for president. Those looks are irresistible, and you know how shallow people are regarding appearances. Of course, you have other things going for you too—being literate really helps.

I would offer to volunteer for you but have decided it would be too big a commitment as I have to keep an eye on Bruno constantly. He is just incorrigible. Can you believe that after our training session last Thursday (when he totally showed off and impressed his trainer, your campaign chairperson), he threw up on me in the car on the way home. Mom felt sorry for him and that he couldn't help it, but I know better. Anyway, he can't be trusted and would probably be an embarrassment as he campaigned door to door.

I will put in good words for you whenever there is opportunity, and you will definitely get our votes.

Sincerely,

Stella (and for Bruno)

Letter 76

Oh. Thank you, Stella (and Bruno). I am sorry your dear mom got all dirty on the way home on Thursday. Those little dogs can be a pain. I have not had a good experience with them myself. It is a good thing that he is handsome, huh?

Veni

PS: Do you have a photo of you and Bruno? If so, I would like to have one. I will put you and Bruno on my dating service! Actually, a girl dog, named Stella (can you believe!) is looking for another husband. She was married to a pit bull named Tank. They got a divorce. Perhaps Bruno? She is a beautiful standard poodle. She likes shorter boy dogs.

Letter 77

Hi, my friends,

Have you heard that I got eighteen thousand hits on my run for president of the United States? It is true. I did!

Now I have some ideas. It is never too late, but this will take some work! I have contacted many of my canine friends and have also spread the word to my horse, donkey, llama, alpaca, cow, sheep (know them well), goats (know some of them as well), turkeys (my friends that I saved at Thanksgiving), lions, monkeys, gorillas, deer, antelopes, elk, tigers, etc. And last but not least, cats. No dogs are allowed to chase cats! If so, they will be thrown out of our campaign. We need all the animals we can get. What do you think. Insects maybe?

I have a demonstration planned! It has to be civil. No ugly protests are allowed! If we do this the right way, we could win the White House. We need to get along. All positive thoughts are encouraged! I can do this with your help. Tell all your friends. *Hope is still alive!*

Just think of all the parties we could have! Dog bones galore!

Letter 78

1. I am hopping on your bandwagon for sure! Love, love, love your picture. When can I pull those cute ears?

Your friend Willow

2. Thanks, Willow. Do you think that you could help with my campaign? I like you (much better than Demi).
3. You bet I can help. Can I move to your place? I cannot stand these puppies another minute! Your friend, Willow
4. Come on over, Willow! I will help find you a husband. Sometimes it takes two to three to find the right one. I hear this from some of Mom's friends. Mom and Dad have been married fifty years. I told everyone that they were old. I was right!

MOM'S VACATION!!

Letter 79

Dear Dem, Levi, and Veni,

Please do not feel sad because I left for eight to nine days. I *will* be home! Mom needed a relaxing vacation. As you know, it has been very stressful for both your dad and I for over a year.

I rushed out (as you know) at six thirty this morning, and just arrived in Klamath Falls, Oregon, at two thirty. I wanted to tell you about my first day on the road all by myself. It felt weird because my two pumik were not in the back seat of my car. It was strange, but I still felt you were there!

So let me tell about my trip so far. Dad will read this to you for your bedtime story tonight.

I stopped for a quick fill up (gas) in Corning, California, and grabbed a half sandwich and iced tea at Starbucks and kept driving. Right after Redding, California, it starts to get really beautiful. Shasta Lake was filled to the brim with bright blue water, and then I spotted Mt. Shasta in all its glory! It is a very tall mountain with snow still on halfway down. What a sight! Veni, do you remember your overnight stay on Mt. Shasta when you spotted one of the Lumerians (the little people who live by the mountain)? This is one of your dad's favorite towns. It is very spiritual, even though you were so frightened.

After two more hours of driving, I saw a sign for Tulelake, California. I do not think you know this, but this is where I grew up as a child. It was population fifteen hundred. It is a farming community. My dad was a potato farmer and shipper. He had a packing shed and designed many of his own equipment. Mom came out of her shell in high school and was a song leader for three years and homecoming queen and won the drama award on graduation day. Her grandmother was a school teacher and a very good artist (and writer).

Tulelake was also the home of the Modoc Indian tribe. There are still writings on the side of the mountains when there was a lake. It has dried up in that area, but there is still a lake where duck hunters go during the season (a little history lesson).

Then on to Klamath Falls, Oregon, only twenty-three miles. This is where your dad and I met a little over fifty-three years ago. It was at a dance. We both loved to dance and still do. It has been a little tough from the time your dad lost his leg from the knee down, but we will do it again! Your dad's mother was an accountant and his dad, a saw filer.

I thought it was time to fill you doggies in on our past. There is much more to come because, Veni, you want to know about all the dogs in the past. I told you about some, but there are many more stories to come!

Love,

Mom

PS: On to Eugene, Oregon, tomorrow to see Aunt Leslie. Veni, I know you think she is a ghost, but you are wrong. She is a special person!

Letter 80

Dear Demi, Levi, and Veni,

To continue, after I left Klamath Falls, Oregon, at 7:30 a.m., my GPS system guided me (you have to learn how to use this, Demi) on a two-lane road on to Medford, Oregon to eventually land me in Eugene, Oregon. But there was a mishap on the way. I was following a *slow* truck and finally got to pass it (I was thrilled), and then all of a sudden, I saw a policeman sitting by the side of the road. I threw on my brakes, but all of a sudden, he was behind me with his light flashing telling me to go to the side of the road and wait for a speeding ticket! He walked over to tell me I was speeding. I was going seventy-three in a fifty-five. I honestly thought the speed limit was sixty-five! I could not find my registration (another offense). I was in big trouble! The policeman was nice in fact. He did not write me up for that speed and did not write me up for no registration (I blamed this on your dad!). He even gave me directions. He was nice but not *nice enough*. I have a radar detector in my car, but guess what! I unplugged it, and *forgot* to plug it back in. *Ugh*!

I arrived in Eugene at eleven thirty in the morning. I unloaded my car, went shopping with Aunt Leslie, and got home just in time to see all the Jackson families for pizza. Sorry, Veni, I know how you miss your pizza from Italy!

We were to leave for Newport, Oregon, in the morning, but Aunt Leslie had a little mishap herself (tell you later), so we did not leave until one in the afternoon, arriving around three. We rushed to our room and unpacked as quickly as we could so we could do our shopping in the little boutiques. It was fun!

Here is another story, doggies. Mom was finishing up in a boutique when Aunt Leslie spotted an older man with three young kids. She heard the kids asking him how far away he lived. He told them one and one half hours. She had a bad feeling about this, so she told me to hurry up! We ran out, got in the car and followed the man and three kids. She got a photo! He kept looking at Aunt Leslie. We thought it was a guilty look! We followed them, and the man kept looking back at us.

We called 911. A. Leslie told them all the details, but they disappeared by the library. I got out of the car to look in the library. They were not there. They disappeared into thin air. I think that he got them in a car and left. It is still bothering us. Not a good feeling! We hope and pray that those three little kids are okay.

Then we stopped and had an iced tea… then a beer (for me) and glass of wine for Aunt Leslie. We stayed at Georgie's for dinner also. *It was the best dinner, guys.* Oh my gosh, we did not know this, but it was a five-star restaurant. I sent a photo to brother Chris telling him it was to die for. He hates it when we say this, but this is the best description!

We are back in our room now, looking for a new place to stay. They have *no air conditioning. Can you believe!* Aunt Leslie made reservations too late. Next time, Mom will be in charge!

We plan to leave tomorrow to Lincoln City. It is another little town by the sea. It is really beautiful here in Newport! There are some interesting people here on the Oregon Coast. I know that you do not know what hippies are, but I will explain later.

Love,

Mom

Letter 81

Dear Demi, Levi, and Veni,

It is now Friday, and thank goodness, we left our motel this morning. You dogs would have melted! We called for a fan, and one hour later (after three calls to the desk), they *finally* brought a fan. Then after they came, we found a fan in the closet. (They should have told us!) We did not mention this because they did not charge us for today (Friday), and took some money off for Thursday. We told them that we were checking out a day early because we were dying of heat stroke in our room. This was absolutely true!

We are now in Lincoln City, Oregon, on the coast again. It is cooler and windier here. But thank goodness, we have a nice room with air conditioning! This city is right on Highway 101. Tons of traffic! Why? It is the kite festival this weekend. Doggies. There are *so many* interesting kites. I know that you would have enjoyed seeing all of them. Dog kites even!

Aunt Leslie and I did some shopping today. This is what we do best! We are professionals, as you (Veni and Levi) know. You two are so good about staying in the dressing rooms with me. Don't tell Dad! Some things are left better unsaid!

It is four, and we are now back in our room. I have to admit that I am drinking an early beer. Yum! Aunt Leslie is take a little snooze because she did not sleep well last night. She was worried about the three little boys I told you about yesterday. We hope and pray that they are all right

Later, we were walking across the street to a Mexican food restaurant. I heard that your dad and aunt Mary had the same food at two. I hope that you are behaving yourselves! Veni, you do have to work on your barking! You do it too often, and too much during the day. Do you want one of those collars? If not, stop it!

Love you, doggies and Dad!

I will keep you informed because we are on our way to Cannon Beach (my favorite!) tomorrow morning. I have to work on Aunt Leslie to get going in the morning. She loves her crossword puzzles. This should *not* happen on vacation!

Love,

Mom

Letter 82

Dear doggies,

We left Lincoln City this morning (Sunday) around eight thirty. Aunt Leslie is not as much a morning person. She likes to sleep in. I am a get up and go person, as you know. I think that she was a little mad at me because I was trying to hurry her. She *does not like this*! She was fine after we got on the road. We went down Highway 101 by the ocean.

It was a beautiful drive! Everything is so *green*! We kept looking for a cafe because we were very hungry. We found a cute little town along the way where we knew we would find a good cafe. It was Rockaway, Oregon. We noticed that there was a little street fair, so we asked a man and his wife if they knew a good restaurant. He said they were from out of town but that he *loved* my hair (I was wearing a black scarf on my head so I did not have to do my hair that morning), and that he liked my earrings. Weird. Until I found out that the street fair was a pirate festival. He thought I was dressed up like a pirate for the festival. I do not think it was a compliment for my attire.

We found a wonderful little cafe on the way to Cannon Beach. It was *so* busy, that we just knew that we made the right choice. *It was so good* that we wanted to drive back every day, even though it was at least an hour away.

We arrived in Cannon Beach around one. Our room was not ready at the Hallmark, so we took off downtown to do what we do best. Shop!

We did the whole town in about three to four hours just as we got a call that our room was ready. It was beer time! I had a Piraat beer. It is pronounced Pirate. Interesting, huh! We relaxed a little, then started looking for a restaurant that was within walking distance so I did not have to drive. I wanted to have a gin, doggies. Not to worry!. I am *not* an alcoholic. We walked to the Wayfarer restaurant.

We were seated in the bar next to a couple who told us that they had just met online three months prior and they were in love! We talked with them throughout our dinner. Rudy was Hawaiian from Seattle, and his girlfriend, Jeri was from Washington also. As we talked, we found Rudy was a real dog lover, so I told him about your book Veni. He bought one. Rudy was so hilariously funny that we could barely eat. We laughed and laughed! As we were leaving, Rudy came to our table to tell us that he bought our dinner. We were flabbergasted! As were leaving, Rudy ran outside yelling, Pam, Pam, Pam. You forgot your glasses! Aunt Leslie and I had another good laugh because this is exactly what your Dad does... Pam, Pam, Pam! I felt like I was home! I thought I was home listening to your dad!

Cannon Beach was so much fun, doggies! We left for Eugene the next morning and arrived about three thirty. I took Aunt Leslie and Uncle Mike out for a nice dinner that night. It was wonderful!. Then straight to bed! Mom did all the driving, so I was a little tired. Pirates have to work very hard on those ships!

Love,

Mom

Letter 83

Dear doggies,

It is now Wednesday. I woke up at four forty-five in the morning. Tuesday night Aunt Leslie had some of the family over for taco soup. We met Mike for lunch, then shopped for groceries until three in the afternoon on Tuesday. We did not have much time, so we cleaned the house, made dinner, and then sat down for a few minutes before everyone came. The last bit of family stayed until eleven or eleven thirty. We all had a great time, but I did not get much sleep.

I tiptoed very quietly out of the house by six or six fifteen. Aunt Leslie has been sleeping off and on all day. She was *worn out*! She calls your mom a hummingbird because she says that I flitter all day long and never sit. Or she calls me an ever-ready battery.

I arrived in (guess where, Veni?) your favorite town, Mt. Shasta. Yes, where the Lumerians live. I am staying at the Tree House Motel, the same place where you heard the Lumerians talking that night when your dad and I were sound asleep. I got here early, at ten forty-five, so I had to go shopping (something I hate) until they called me at one thirty when they had a room ready. Don't tell Dad, but I did find a small (and I mean small) pendant of Mt. Shasta—a reminder of you and your dad. Your dad *loves* Mt. Shasta!

It is time for dinner, doggies. I am hungry and tired. I have to admit that I was going to have a salad for lunch, but opted for garlic French fries… the best I have *ever* had!

Love to your dad, Mary, and you doggies! See you tomorrow.

Love,

Mom

PS: It was *so nice* for your Dad's cousin Mary to come all the way from Arizona to stay with you and your dad so Mom could take some time off. I can hardly wait to see all of you tomorrow!. Woo-hoo!

Letter 84

Dear Veni,

I thought you might want a photo of the bistro where Aunt Leslie, Uncle Mike, your dad, and I had dinner the night that you tried your escape from the car. You almost got Aunt Leslie killed trying to save you from the traffic. You ran to the grassy area, remember? Mom had to run across the street in the dark and give you a down signal. You hit the ground, thank God, and I told you to stay (you did, thank God). Then I picked you up and put you back in the car. You almost gave your mom and dad a heart attack!

Mom

Letter 85

To all my friends,

Mom arrived home on Thursday, after a long vacation—too long! She was gone for eight days. She said she needed a break from us doggies, especially me. My heart was broken!

Dad's cousin Mary stayed with all of us. She is really nice, but I think Mom should have stayed home. She wrote to us every day, and Dad read us her letters at bedtime. This was very nice of her, but I feel that she should have taken me with her. She did think about it but decided that she needed real alone time. Not fair!

We were *so excited* when she arrived home, but she sort of ruined the excitement by grooming us right after she unpacked the car. Levi and I were afraid of this and were hoping she would be too tired... *not*!

Mom and Dad had a Fourth of July party yesterday. I hated every second of it. The kids screamed as they jumped in the pool. I spent my time in the doggie bar. You do know that there is a dog bar dedicated to my deceased brother, Charley. I asked Mom if she could put some wine in my dog bowl, but she refused Next time, I will just help myself.

Happy Independence Day to everyone. My run for mayor of Chualar is going well. I will keep you informed, but some more votes would help!

Love,

Veni

PS: I did hear from my donors for my presidential run. They are rethinking their decision to take me out. I will keep you informed!

Letter 86

To all my voters!

As you might recall, both parties are trying to get me to drop out of the race. I called my two attorneys, Johnny Collieran and Christopher Doxie. Here is what they suggested

They are contacting every canine in all the states. The press has not told you, but I am doing *very* well! It is an embarrassment to all involved that I have over 30 million votes. The delegates are the problem! We are in the process of taking care of this.

We have had many rallies. I have friends in every state. Johnny suggested that my campaign managers go to every precinct and knock on every door! All dogs will go on a hunger strike if their loved ones do not vote for me. (Not to worry, we will be sneaking you food!)

I need all of my doggie supporters to vote for me! I promise to have your favorite treats in the White House. It will soon become doggie house! The world will be a better place again

Veni Jackson

Veni for President 2016

Vote for me! We can do it!

PS: I have many other species of animals, insects, etc., working for my run also.

Letter 87

Worn out!

To all of my friends and Veni's friends,

To put it bluntly, we had the weekend from hell! My husband John's aunt passed on in Medford, Oregon. We left on Thursday, went to the funeral on Friday, and planned on going to Klamath Falls, Oregon, for the burial on Saturday. After a call from our dog sitter, we rushed home on Saturday burdened with very little sleep on Friday night. Veni disappeared! Not to be found. She jumped the fence and was seen but just kept running from Friday afternoon until 5:30 a.m. on Saturday. We had many friends at the house along with our oldest son, Chris. Chris tried to tackle her after many hours of spotting her, to no avail. She was too fast!

I was, to say the very least, *sick*! I cried all night, got John up at 5:00 a.m., and told him we were heading home, which is an eight-and-a-half-hour drive. I mention to John that after I hugged her, I was going to kill her! We got a call from our dog sitter suggesting that we immediately take her to the emergency vet because her eye was swollen. I have *never* seen so many fox tails on one dog in my life! Now I was *totally* sick. We rushed her to the vet and waited until they checked her out. I asked them not to shave her because I was determined to groom her when we got home. They found three fox tails in her eye and in every single orifice of her body. We went home with a cone, along with two different drops for her eye, and pain medication. She was also limping because she had cracked her pads.

I spent about three hours working on the fox tails and had to cut some out of her chest. They were in tightly matted balls. I then carried her into our bedroom and placed her on John's lap while I vacuumed and vacuumed. I am still (every day) finding fox tails in every room in our house.

Moral of the story (she will tell you a different story): she was afraid and looking for me.

From Veni. Here is the truth! I knew that I *had* to get to Indiana to work on delegates and votes for my presidency! I ran all the way to Highway 101 and stuck out my paw to all the truck drivers for a ride. I could not find any of them heading to Indiana. They offered to take me as far as Arizona. I have been there (if you remember), and I do not want to go back! So after many hours, I decided to go home. I am sorry about upsetting all my friends, but I do not have much time to gather votes. I still have a chance. I *will* take California! I have millions of write-in votes, which none of the media will cover. I will be in the debates with Hillary and Donald. I can talk faster than both of these candidates, and if they say something that I do not like, I know how to lift my lips and growl!

Vote for me!

Veni for President

Letter 88

My dearest Veni,

I am so sorry that I have been so quiet lately. I have read your words, but I was in too much of a weakened state to reply. Now, I must reply.

I remember your escapade in April when you decided to try to make the great escape when your parents were in Oregon. Girlie, you scared the pants off of your family. What in the world were you thinking? It was hard to feel sorry for you about all of the thistles lodged in your hair. Yikes! You need to calm your jets, girlie, and look at the long term. *Please*! Consider longevity. If you don't straighten out and fly right, you will not be around in the near future. I say this as a beloved relative. We want you around to have family fun. Do you get it? Okay.

Also, I think I need to have a family conference when I come down. You have been misbehaving, and now there are physical changes. Who knows what that will bring?

Have you considered going holistic and seeing a doggie shrink? Dear Veni, there is time for your redemption. Please, please, consider your options.

I am weary, and I am sure I haven't done my punctuation correctly. However, it is because I love you and needed to have you to embrace life on your own. You are growing up, and you must find your path of success. Be the one that makes a difference in the lives of others. You can do it. I am your greatest cheerleader, Veni.

Now I must sign off. Remember, I will always be near in thought and prayer.

Love always,

Jude

Letter 89

Dear Friends,

I am certain you all remember that I jumped the fence when Mom and Dad were in Oregon just because it was imperative that I get to Indiana to work on my campaign. My parents were *very* upset with me! I wish that they understood how important it is to run for president for heaven's sake! I now have a new collar just like Levi's. Levi likes to jump fences also. I think his collar is *ugly*, and now I have the same ugly collar. And guess what? I hate it! It is not only ugly, but it also makes me jump back from the gates. Mom has to go out with me to go potty now. I am tiptoeing around the grass. I do not trust anything in the backyard now. Some monster inside my new collar tries to scare me! I did not deserve this. However, Mom and Dad disagree. My life has changed forever! Boo-hoo, sniff, sniff! By the way, perfect Demi does not have one of these ugly collars. She would never do *anything* that was *not* perfect!

And then Demi tells me every day that black lives matter! I hear this *every day* and that I must make this part of my campaign. I agree that black lives matter, but look at all the people and dogs that are different colors. Red, yellow, brown, white, pink, gray, and blue. (I saw a lady with blue hair.) Demi thinks that it is all about her, but don't you agree that all lives matter? It is just not all about Demi!

Another bad thing happened this week. Mom got two doggie tents for the backseat. We no longer have freedom like we did before. It is all Levi's fault! He jumps around, whines, and barks all the way to the main road. I hide on the floor or try to get in the front seat with Mom because he frightens me. Levi fought like a bucking bronco when Mom put him in the tent. I, on the other hand, crawled up and lay down. I wanted to make her happy because I have been in so much trouble. Levi is *not* happy, but to be honest, I like it because I do not have to listen to him now. Whew!

Not a good week for the pumik at the Jackson household.

Love,

Veni

Veni for President

Letter 90

To all my wonderful supporters,

I have some very bad news about my campaign. I just received a registered letter from the government animal community. I had many donors from this community, but they have decided that there is not enough money to further support my campaign. And they say that I need a little more experience in government. I am crushed! I have as much experience as the other two candidates as far as I am concerned! Sniff, sniff! I had it all planned. Levi was going to be my VP because he does anything I tell him to do. Demi was going to be secretary of state so I could get her out of town. Then I was going to have many doggie parties at the White House and invite all of you plus many other animals. The wine and beer would flow, plus any kind of food that would make all of you happy. However, chicken, beef, and lamb will not be available. Just think how this would make our cow, chicken, and sheep friends feel.

So I am running for mayor of Chualar, which I just posted. I am asking for your votes! This will give me the experience they say I need to run for president in four years unless whoever wins gets impeached. Then I will step right in!

I thank you for all your support and hope that you will send in a vote for mayor of Chualar.

Veni Jackson

Letter 91

Dear, Pam,

Just got e-mail from Veni asking what spayed is. She was so excited because she thought it had something to do with a crown and jewels. She was appalled when I explained it to her. I'd keep your keys on you at all times. I think she is planning an escape.

Clint

Letter 92

To all my doggie friends,

About three weeks before Mom went on vacation, I had to have surgery! I did not want to tell you because it had something to do with my private parts. Some people told me that they did not like my hips. How dare they! My boy dog friends love my hips!

A doctor had to take my private parts, which means that I cannot be a show dog. My mom was very upset, but I am not. I did not like those judges going over my body, so all is okay with me. I really like herding and nose work way better!

I had to wear one of those horrible plastic things around my neck. I hated it! Then my new scar got itchy. But I learned how to take care of this. I scratched my tummy with my rear feet. Mom got upset with me, so put me in doggie diapers. All was *very* embarrassing! It was a very long two weeks!

I know what you are going to say, Hoover. You love the fact that I now have a scar. Mine will not be as visible as yours though. Too bad that your scar is right on your nose!

Love,

Veni

Letter 93

Hi, Veni,

First off, I don't have a scar on my nose. I have a tattoo under my eye. You will have that scar forever, and most male dogs will be looking for it.

I still love you with or without your scar.

Hoover

Letter 94

Thanks, Hoover. I think? I love you too. I think?

Love,

Veni

Letter 95

Hi Veni,

It's been awhile since we wrote. Things have just been so busy in my household. My brave dad changed jobs last year and is now camp commander at the Gabilan Conservation Camp. This means he is helping fight fires with inmates now! He is working very hard on the Soberanes fire burning in Monterey County. Each day he watches over eight hundred inmates trying to save our beautiful lands and homes. My mom has been told he won't be home for thirty more days.

Since Dad is gone, I am now the man of the house. Today is my fourth birthday too. My birthday wish is to get close to my lovely-smelling mom and auntie, but I know Mom won't let that happen. She never did find me a girlfriend. I guess she doesn't want me to be truly happy. I heard your mom cramped your style too. Moms just don't understand we need companionship of the furry kind. Being man's best friend just isn't enough sometimes.

Mom hasn't been letting me play outside lately either, something about hawks carrying me away. This country life is not for the faint of heart. Danger lurks in every corner. You must be brave to live here. Good thing I have my marine corps background to guide me.

I have been bored without Dad here, so I have been listening to the TV a lot. I hear a lot of "lock her up" and "be sacred, so very scared." I notice Mom rolling her eyes and asking, "Why isn't it November yet?" Perhaps this is your time, Veni. Political office may be your calling. I would be happy to serve in your campaign too. Our slogan could be "Pom-Pumi's Unite"!

I enclosed a new picture of myself. Mom says I am still as handsome as ever. Write back soon.

Semper Fi,

Gunny

Letter 96

Hi Gunny,

I certainly am glad that your dad is safe and will continue to be safe. I thought about volunteering myself but am busy running for mayor of Chualar. I guess that you did not hear that my doggie donors told me that I had to give up my run for president. They were running out of money and also felt I needed some more experience. I was crushed! But I think that I will be mayor of Chualar. Check Facebook. You can actually vote! And this week, I will have a poster at the post office and a tablet asking for votes. I will make it and then run for president in four years. I will still be young!

Love,

Veni

Letter 97

Wow, Chualar mayor—that's impressive! My mom is super mean. I can't use Facebook. She says its full of trolls and identity thieves. I think it must be full of pictures of girl dogs she doesn't want me to know about.

It's sad you and Jeb had to give up your run for president. Lack of funds is a big deal. I figured your mom would have chipped in more. Our parents are just so cheap sometimes. It's all about them and their bills.

I think you will enjoy being mayor more anyway. You can still live at home. No moving to a big White House where you can't even potty on the lawn.

If you win, Veni, you might need an assistant. I am available.

Gunny

Letter 98

Dear Friends,

Today is August 28, 2016, which is a day that will be forever embedded in my memory

It is Sunday. All of we dogs were fed first as always. Mom sat down to eat her yogurt, Levi was lying right next to her (Mommy's boy), Demi was perched on the back of the couch (Queenie), and I was sitting on the couch. I picked up the *Canine Times* to relax and read, but something made my jaw drop! Right on the front page was an article about the National Animal Association—the one and only that was promoting and financing my campaign.

Here is what it said.

It has been discovered that the National Animal Association had a visit from one of the campaign managers of two people who are running for president. The CEO will not tell us who it was and said that he never will! It was to talk about Miss Veni Jackson's run for the presidency.

They did not like the fact that Miss Jackson was getting so many votes. She was taking votes away from them, they said. They told the CEO that he had to stop financing her campaign, and that if he did not, they would be forced to refuse food and water to all the farm animals! They talked about horses, cows, sheep, pigs, goats, ducks, etc.

Written by Darcie Weiner

OMD! How despicable and disgusting! I yelled at Mom and Dad to read the article. I immediately got on the phone to make some calls. I called the Hound Dog Association and the Sporting Breed Association, and all the dogs that are proficient in nose work. They are on their way to both campaign headquarters. They are going to sniff out the situation.

I then called the Herding Breed Association and the Working Breed Association. I included some in the non-sporting, like the standard poodle (yes, I hate to admit that they are smart), pit bulls, and some in the Toy Breed Association. We are going to Washington, DC, to *protest*! I asked the police dogs, pit bulls, and Rottweilers to police the protest.

This is the reason I wanted to run for your president. I wanted to work for you and the animal community. These people would do *anything* for a vote! They are a disgrace and perhaps need to be put down!

Veni Jackson

Now running for Mayor of Chualar. Vote for me!

PS: *I will be back in 2020.*

My Herding Career!

Letter 99

To all my friends,

Many of you know that I qualified for my herding certificate, but you have not heard about my weekend. Mom's friend Anna went with us. I love Anna, so I was excited! I even slept on her bed some of the time. She is fun!

My other friend and mentor, Clint, was there to cheer me on. However, I think that he played a trick on me. He told them to give me sheep that like to run back to the gate. I got to practice a little bit on Friday before my test on Saturday and Sunday. I did not know what to do. Mr. Clint told me that I had to learn! Well! I hope he gets some tough sheep himself someday soon!

I went in to do my herding trail around eleven on Saturday. *It was hot!* Mom threw some water on me to cool me down. My judge was very nice. He qualified me. Mom and I were so excited! Then she and Aunt Anna decided to go to a *huge* shopping center. I hated every minute of it. Everywhere we went, we got stopped. "OM gosh," they would say. "This is the cutest dog I have ever seen. What mix is she? Those are the cutest ears. Did you have to do surgery on them?" All the same questions, over and over and over! Mom could not do any shopping. I am sure Dad was very happy!

We arrived at the herding trail about the same time on Sunday. Aunt Anna likes to sleep in, but Mom gets up way too early according to Aunt Anna! We had a new judge that day. Mr. Clint got first and second place on his two border collies on Friday and Saturday. He said that they did well on Sunday also, but the judge did not even give him a qualifying score. He was *not happy*! Mom was nervous about this judge now!

I went in, and I had to pee and poop. Things happen, as you know. After all, I am a dog! This was not *disqualifying* however. But I had to catch up with Mom and the sheep, and she did not trust me to go slow. She kept telling me to slow down. The judge qualified me after she told Mom that she talks too much. Mr. Clint did stick up for Mom though. Thanks, Mr. Clint

There is one thing though, Mr. Clint, that Mom would like to talk to you about. Even at the herding trail, so many people came over to tell Mom that I was adorable. You know what Mr. Clint said? He told Mom that she got me just because she likes attention. *Can you believe!* Mom thinks that he is jealous!

Mr. Clint, I will come visit you so you can have some attention that I believe you need. I have to admit that I am adorable!

Love,

Veni

PS: I know that one of my boyfriends sent me these flowers, but there was no name. Was it you, Hoover?

Letter 100

Congrats to you, Veni. A big *woo-hoo*! Bring out the marching band and celebrate in the streets. Your picture in front of the fireplace is quite regal and fitting. Hopefully, you have put in a request for your favorite meal!

Love,

Jude

Letter 101

Hi Veni,

I'm so proud of you! Congratulations on your hard work.

I wanted to tell you about a new game that my parents and I play every evening. Take one Greenie. Cut it into six small pieces. Obey their sit and stay command. Let them hide the pieces. Get the okay signal, and then just devour them all. What they don't realize is that I'm peeking around the corner in the kitchen and know exactly where the Greenies have been hidden. Sure is fun as they still think I'm the smartest dog in town. Keep up the good work!

Toby

Letter 102

Yes, Veni! Way to go! Love you so much! And love your mom too. I had the greatest time (even if Mom gets crazy about getting places two hours early) and can't wait to be with you again for another adventure and also get to visit with my new friend Clint.

Love and kisses,

Your new roommate

Letter 103

Hi, Veni,

It's me, Chesty. It's been a long time since I wrote. I figured now was a good time to catch up. I am finally back home after joining the marines. Mom decided I needed a different upbringing, so I was the brave one that packed my sea bag and headed off for a three-year adventure.

A lot has changed since I left home. It seems Gunny, my brother, thinks he is in charge now. I know he has been to combat. I heard him talking about his war injury, but I still think I am tougher. You see, I actually left home, unlike that momma's boy. While he did his military service one weekend a month and two weeks a year, I was traveling the globe protecting you every day.

Now that I am back, I tried to tell Mom that I don't like the rations she is trying to feed me. I also don't like any of the dishes she expects me to eat off of. I also have to be let out a lot to relieve myself. I make Dad stand outside with a flashlight usually around 3:00 a.m. We check for any outdoor security threats while my brother Gunny stays inside. I think the bravery gene may have skipped him.

As I settle into civilian life, I plan on letting my hair grow out. Mom says it isn't a good look for me to be shaved. I think this is just a ploy from Mom to trim me like a topiary just like when I was a kid.

Well, we should really catch up soon. Next time you head over to see Clint, you should stop by. I am working on my PTSD right now, but Mom expects my full recovery shortly.

That's the latest from SJB, San Juan Bautista.

Hoorah,

Chesty

Letter 104

Chesty. You poor thing! I have never admitted this to anyone, but I know that you will keep this to yourself. I am afraid of the dark! Every morning at four thirty when Mom and Dad get up, they let us out to go potty. I stick my head out, but I do not go out. I am afraid. I wait until it is lighter. I think I am the smartest one. What if there are creatures out there? Levi is always barking at something! Please keep this to yourself. Do not even tell your brother! I know that I am a "Dear Veni," so this is truly embarrassing!

Love,

Veni

Letter 105

Hi, Veni,

It seemed like a good time to write as I just woke Mom up guarding the house at 2:00 a.m. Mom says I am a little miffed now that my brother Chesty has returned from his tour of duty. Dad named Chesty after a famous Marine. He left for a military life three years ago. It seems his tour of duty is over now, and mom says he is back home for good.

I had no say in any of this. I have been the only man of the house besides Dad since he left. I thought all my problems were gone, but here he is back again. Mom has been paying extra attention to Chesty since his service ended. She said he needs adjustment time. I tried my hardest to get him to play, but he just stands there. I imagine he learned that from Demi. It's almost like he is too good to play! I thought that was only a poodle trait.

Now that Chesty is settling in, Mom talks constantly about how the marines shaved his hair. All I hear is, "Poor dog how could the barber do that to your hair?" I think Chesty looks like an Ewok with his haircut.

Thank goodness, I am follicle gifted and remain the most handsome dog at home. I know you can relate. Demi will never be half as cute as you are!

I plan on heading back to bed now the security threat from a pair of headlights seems to be resolved.

Semper Fi,

Gunny

Letter 106

Oh, Gunny, it is *so good to hear from you*! I am sorry to hear that you have someone in your family like Demi. *Ugh*!

Letter 107

I understand Veni, and I won't tell anyone about the boogie man living in the dark that may be out to get you! I have my own fears too. Now they include dog dishes, kibble, the garbage being taken out, TV, playing with other dogs, and being left home alone.

Mom says when I grew up, none of these things bothered me. Now after my military life, I have issues, as Mom puts it. I am a little embarrassed too. Maybe we can work on our overcoming these things together. After all, marines and herding dogs are very brave.

Letter 108

Hi, Veni,

The parental units are in Hawaii for two weeks, and they left us fur kids with the sitter. I figured this was a good time to write on election eve. I have been getting the sitter up every night between 3:00 and 5:00 a.m. I think she is pretty mad at me for it. I heard her telling my mom. I was hoping this would make Mom come home, but so far nothing. I think the sister is making my food portions smaller just to get back at me.

Chesty is still here, and we are getting to know each other again. So far I know he can pee farther than me as we have a daily contest, much to Mom's dislike. Mom says Chesty isn't fat anymore. He lost one pound in a month. Mom gives herself a lot of credit on this one as he was trying to complain about the two squares a day served here by not eating. It just didn't work out for him. Mom even got him to eat out of a dog dish. I tell you that woman plays Jedi mind tricks on us. She is kind of incredible.

Mom said the Hollywood folks who have my auntie Luci called. Aunt Luci is going to be in a big car commercial. I heard Mom telling them about Chesty. Now Hollywood wants him too! This isn't fair, Veni. I am the most handsome dog here. Why don't they want me? Dad is really sad at the thought of Chesty leaving home to become a movie star, but Mom thinks it might be just what he needs.

I would enjoy stardom too. Instead I wait for my girlfriend that is never coming, and now I am destined to be a bachelor until the end of time. I plan on being mad when Mom gets home so I can tell her it's my time to be famous and meet a cute girl. I hope she listens.

Gunny

Letter 109

My Dear Gunny,

I feel that there are three reasons you are waking up between 3:00 a.m. and 5:00 a.m.

Number 1: *You are starving!* They must feed you, for heaven's sake!

Number 2: You want to go outside to pee. I know you are working on distance!

Number 3: You are thinking about your plan for Hollywood. Why Chesty?

I met a few producers when I went to Hollywood to pitch for my book. I will try to contact them. As a matter of fact, I think they need *me* also. I am, after all, beautiful! Perhaps you need to help me with my new job as mayor? I would bet that we will both become famous.

Love,

Veni

PS: You do know that my parents were gone for fifteen days? We were left *alone*, but there is another side of the story. I will write later!

Johnny Collierun

Letter 110

To Johnny Collieran, Attorney at Law

Dear Mr. Collieran,

Just to refresh your memory, you took our case pro bono about a year ago or so, Demi (a standard poodle), Levi (a pumi), and me, Veni Jackson. You got us out of jail for driving without a license. You even got our jail time expunged. We were felons, but no longer. This gave me the right to run for mayor of Chualar, California, I won with 350 votes. The ceremony will be sometime in December.

This is the reason I am writing. I would like you to be my attorney general. I am truly sorry to say that I cannot afford to offer a salary. I am totally broke! Any extra money I make goes to a man named Mr. Clint for herding practice.

Please let me know as quickly as possible. If you decide that you do not want the job, I will have to get in touch with Christopher Doxie, or send Levi to law school.

Thank you,

Veni Jackson

Mayor of Chualar

Writer of "Dear Veni"

Owner of a herding degree, with ribbons

Letter 111

Ms. Veni Jackson, major of Chualar,

It would be my pleasure to serve your administration as attorney general. With all due respect to Christopher Doxie, he would be better suited to serve you as chief of police. He specialized in finding varmints.

Again, congratulations on the election!

Johnny Collieran

Attorney at law

Letter 112

My name is Sparky, and we've never met, but I have admired you from afar. Let me tell you about myself.

I am a dachshund, born in a farm in a place called Hollister. I was almost the last puppy to leave, but I am glad I went to my home. My human mom, Lola, took good care of me, and I had two human pups and several humans to love me. We lived for a while in a town called Green Field. Later we were joined by two more dachshund pups, Lady and Sadie. They didn't look anything like me. My human says I am cream and long haired. Lady is black and tan, and Sadie my mom calls a dapple, whatever that means.

I love giving kisses. That, and eating, are my two favorite things in the world. Well, I also like to get loose and play a fun game of catch the puppy. One time at PetSmart I bolted out the door and ran all the way to the end of the shopping center before they caught me. That was so much fun! Anyway, Mom takes me to the nursing homes sometimes, and I get to meet and kiss a lot of people. It's a place where lots of people need kisses. We moved to Soledad while I was still a pup, and they have a nursing home there we visited sometimes.

Through the years I have slowed down and had some back issues. Mom took me to that dreaded place called the vet. They gave me some white things that tasted nasty. I spit them out as often as I could. Right next door, I got to go see a lady named Becky, and she used a funny thing on my back. The humans called it laser therapy. It did make me feel better. But the last week or so, my human thought my back was acting up again. She didn't know until we went to see Dr. Chaney that I had a very bad infection. They gave me one of those dreaded shots and more nasty pills to take. But overnight I got worse, and I had to go home with Dr. Chaney for the night. I can't eat. It makes me sick. My eyes and my ears are yellow, and I heard my mom say I would be going to the Rainbow Bridge today. Maybe I will meet you there some day. My mom is crying, but I don't have the energy left to even give her a kiss. It's time for me to go, but I wanted to let you know I admired you. Take care of your humans.

Sparky Smith

12-13-2003 to 11-12-2016

In God We Trust

Letter 113

Dear Sparky,

With tears in my little pumi eyes, I have something to tell you. Did you know that once you meet God, he takes you by the paw to meet all you brothers, sisters, and human relative and friends in heaven? And you will notice that you are no longer sick. No sickness is allowed in heaven! They do take you to the doggies' parlor. They give you a bath, including a flea dip. No fleas are allowed in heaven (even though I am certain that you did not have any). They just have to be certain!

Then comes the best part. God guides you to the dachshund palace. Every doggie has their own palace—even the mixed breeds. The mixed breeds have the most beautiful palace of all because they are special in God's eyes.

Tell your mom to dry her eyes because you are happy! All the sickness is gone.

Love,

Veni

PS: Tell are my brothers, sisters, and human relatives hello for me. They will know who you are. I will see you someday myself.

Love,

Veni

Mayor of Chualar

Letter 114

To all my boyfriends, Hoover, Toby, Gunny, and Chesty.

I have a new boyfriend by the name of Louie!

Louie is right up there at the top now. He owns a jewelry store. Whoopee! I just offered Louie a place in my cabinet. He accepted. He will be my secretary of agriculture. He is French, so he will be checking all the wine grapes also. He likes his wine! And my dad is excited because Louie has offered to check the produce Dad sells. This position is called bird dog, even though this is beneath Louie. He likes to be admired but does not like to get his little feet dirty. I am certain he will be wearing mud boots and sunglasses.

Louie would be a catch because I *love* diamonds, and Hoover has always refused to buy me one. But let's talk about Louie! As I watch him, I see that he checks out *all* the girl dogs. I am quite sure that he is a Don Juan. Not a good prospect for a husband. I know he thinks I am beautiful, but could I ever trust him? And… there is another big problem. What is Louie going to do when I go out to herd sheep in the mud? He will be watching me, sitting on his gold throne and smoking a cigar with his bow tie! No. This may not work But he could give me a diamond collar just because.

What do you think, my friends?

Love,

Veni

I will send a photo of Louie

Tippy

Letter 115

Dear Pam and Veni,

I am certainly honored that you asked me to be in your cabinet serving as chief of police. I may be small, but I have very good hearing and terrific eyes. I don't miss a trick! I'm hoping I will get to wear a vest with a badge with my name on it! Tippy Dalman, chief of police. Please keep me notified when trouble arises in Chualar. I'll be ready to go! Looking forward to meeting all the other cabinet members!

Julie and Tippy

Letter 116

Tippy, so glad you wrote!

I am going to Chualar tomorrow to check things out. Perhaps you will get a call. I am so happy that you are polishing your badge because I have a feeling we are going to need you soon. I can grab them with my teeth, and you can use your gun. You do have one, right? It is okay because you are an officer of the law. You are lucky. I have to use my teeth! I would rather have a gun because it really hurts my teeth when I have to bite. There are a few coyotes in Chualar just in case you are not aware, so we have to be careful, Tippy!

Love,

Veni

I will call soon.

Letter 117

To all my friends,

Another Thanksgiving has come and gone, thank goodness! My turkey friends are getting smarter every year. I tell them to head to the hills at least three weeks ahead of time now. I have received many letters thanking me for saving their lives. I feel it so unfair that this has become a custom in the United States! I wrote a letter to the president of the United States about this horrible custom. He disagreed. He told me that he loves turkey. Well, if he loves them so much, he should not eat them, don't you agree? This is a disgrace! Vegetables should be a Thanksgiving custom. Mom agrees. She made a vegetable salad that was delicious. I need some votes from my doggie friends if you agree. We need to change this horrible custom!

Another complaint. We three dogs were left home alone! Levi and I had to stay in our crates, but perfect Demi got to stay out in her usual spot on the bed! Just like the queen she is. We did not get anything special to eat either. No stuffing, no dessert, no vegetables, no sweet potatoes, and no mashed potatoes and gravy. Nope. Just the same old thing. Dry food, a tiny bit of canned food, dinovite (have to have this awful stuff), and to top it off, fish oil thrown down our throats in pill form. We get so tired of the same old thing!

I will not tell you how many hours we had to stay in our crates because Mom and Dad would probably have to go to jail. I will put it this way. They got home, let us out to go potty (my bladder was *so full*), and then they went to bed! What a wonderful day. I am still waiting for my ticket to Italy, Auntie!

Love,

Veni

Soon to be mayor of Chualar!

Letter 118

Hi, everyone,

This is Cookie. She does my mom's nails, and mine. She is *so nice* and loves Levi and me. Levi gets in Mom's lap and helps Cookie with Mom's nails She just got back from Hawaii, and I ask, why didn't she take me? I am the one that really needs a vacation! I think it is because her husband, Andy, only likes their own dogs. He should give me a chance, right? I would not bother him anyway. I would stay

right with Cookie! I might try to get some of his pasta. I think he is Italian! Maybe he could get me a ticket to Italy?

Veni

PS: She voted for me for mayor.

Letter 119

Hi Veni. My name is Thomas, and I am Demi's naughty grandnephew. Just wanted to let you know that I *love* turkey, vegetables, and anything edible (even if it is plastic, wood, cloth, glass, or metal). I have been to the vet twice in three months for stomach x-rays. My parents say that I won't get a Christmas stocking. I don't know what that is as I was only born in December of last year and was too young to remember. I feel bad for you, Veni. Spending a lot of time in a crate is *no fun*. However, I can move my crate all over the kitchen. That is *fun*. I have ruined the flooring doing this. My parents say they have never had a poodle like me. Do you think I was switched at birth and should have been a pumi?

Love,

Thomas

Letter 120

Dear Thomas,

You must get over the turkey thing! They just made me vice president of the Turkey Association of America. Your mom needs to have a serious talk with you!

Thomas, are you related to Elsie, the poodle that found a home with my mom's sister-in-law? If so, I know the reason you are a little brat! She has chewed up three C-paks (her dad's machine that he uses at night to breathe), three of his reading glasses, two of her mom's reading glasses, books, toilet paper (I love it too), their bedspread, the couch, and one of his best bows, including the arrows. He made them himself! He said that he now knows why they looked for a home for Elsie. They say that it is a good thing she is so pretty!

I have to admit, Thomas, that she stayed at our house for three days before she went to her new home in Oregon. They all think that a part of me (Veni) entered her body before she left. I do not think this theory is fair, do you?

Anxious to meet you. Would you send a photo please? I bet you are handsome!

Veni Jackson

Dad's Leg Was Stolen

#1

To all my friends,

As some of you know, a doctor in Redwood City, California, stole half of my dad's leg! I have called my doggie attorney in San Jose, California, Johnny Collieran, and he has promised to find him and charge him with grand theft. Johnny is one of the best attorneys in the United States, so that doctor better start looking for his own attorney. I know this will go to trial. Let's face it, Dr. Z is in *major* trouble!

In the meantime, my poor dad has to use a walker or a wheelchair. He is waiting for his fake leg. I am waiting for Dr. Z to give Dad back his own leg that he has in a secret hiding place! I am heading to Redwood City with Levi and Demi to do a search. I took a nose work class, so I will be sniffing around the doctor's office and his home.

Our friend from Germany (pant, pant!) Leopold is visiting again. He is so handsome! Avery, who is seven years old, even gets shy when she sees him. But she will say that she wants him to stay at her house.

I am upset with Leopold though. He took two of *my* tennis balls to put on Dad's walker. I do think that he should have gone to the store to buy them, not steal them from me. They do not even match for heaven's sake! Dad's tennis balls should look new! My tennis balls have teeth marks in them. I miss them already. I tried to jump on the table to take them back, but Mom caught me!

It may take me a day or two to speak to Leopold, but I know I will not last long. Demi flirts with him every day. I do not want him to forget about *me*!

Love,

Veni

#2

Dear Miss Veni Jackson,

First, I want to offer my condolences about your dad's leg. I have been working on your project night and day. I am sorry it has taken such a long time. I do not have a very good report, I am sorry to say.

Yes. Dr. Z did steal your dad's leg! I know that you took a nose work class, but I felt it was better to hire some bloodhounds from the San Francisco police department. We sent them in the middle of the night to Dr. Z's office and his home. He has a beautiful home near the bay. Herein lies the problem. We did not find any sign of your dad's leg! In looking into his past, we found that he steals *many* legs—so many, in fact, that it is almost impossible to count. We broke into his office and found literally thousands of pieces of paperwork on amputations. We feel that he wanted to keep this on the QT but made the mistake of writing everything down. He obviously enjoys it!

Dr. Z does deserve jail time for sure, but in fact, we have no proof. We could not find your dad's leg, or any other legs in fact. I did mention that he lives by the bay, so this is our conclusion. We met his dog, a Lab. As you know, Labs love to swim. His Lab, we found, has many friends in the sea. We are positive that he shared all those legs with his friends, never to be seen again.

We are so sorry, Veni! We tried our best, but I have to tell you something. We have a private detective watching him at all times, and we have also alerted the police department. They are keeping their eye on him. He does not know, so he will get caught and prosecuted one day very soon. This is when we will find the truth about your dad.

In the meantime, it will not be long now before your dad gets his fake leg. He will be fine, so wipe the tears. You will have to help him for a while, and then one day soon, he will be as good as new! Those treats that he sneaks to you, Levi, and Demi are in your near future!

Take care of yourself,

Johnny Collieran, esq.

Christopher Doxie esq.

#3

Hi, friends!

I am sure that you remember that Dr. Z stole my dad's leg and neglected to return it. This is an update. Christopher Doxie and Johnny Collieran's private detective *never could* find it. It is in the ocean with all the rest of the legs that he took! We are all hoping and praying that he will go to jail someday. It will happen! It is just a matter of time

Because Dad only has one leg plus a fake one, he does not feed us anymore in the morning at four thirty. He used to let us all out to go potty, then let us run down the long hall, allowing us to bark and jump until the food bowls hit the floor. Mom has to do both feedings now. We do not like the fact that she stays in bed longer than Dad, but we have learned how to deal with it and most importantly, what to do about it.

We still try to sneak out with Dad, but he tells us to get back on the bed. We do. Mom usually gets up at 5:30 or 6:00 a.m. We know how to read the clock. When it approaches five thirty, I move in to kiss her all over her face. I do not allow Levi to do this. This is *my* job! Levi's job is to put his paws on Mom's tummy just where her bladder is. I see her trying to move on her side. If this does not work, Levi flings his whole body on her tummy. He weighs thirty-five pounds. I still kiss her face.

She tries *not* to open her eyes or talk, because if this happens, we go full force. I kiss harder, and Levi *stands* on her stomach!

This always works. At this point, Levi and I are not her favorite dogs! What does perfect Demi do? She stays at the bottom of the bed and never moves until Mom gets out of bed. I really dislike her! Mom kisses her more than Levi and me every morning and tells her how much she loves and appreciates her. *Uhh*!

I thought that all my doggie friends needed a suggestion when your Mom and Dad want to sleep in on a Sunday morning. For all my very small doggie friends like Toby, Chesty and Gunny, Harley and Lexi, Shilo, and my new friend, Toby, I suggest a bag full of sand. Hope this helps!

Love you,

Veni

Toby

#4

Dear Mr. Toby,

My mom is very sorry that she had to cancel your lesson, but there was a reason. My dad got a huge gift yesterday! He was given a leg, but it is fake! Did you know that his doctor took his leg and did not give it back! My attorneys found out that he does this sort of thing quite often. We also heard that he is going in for major therapy. He finally acknowledges that he has a serious problem. It is a very unusual illness. It is called leganitis. There is a class-action law suit going on now with this particular doctor. I am sorry, but I cannot give you his name.

Getting back to the reason Mom could not make training today. Dad's appointment to get his fake leg was at four thirty in Monterey. My brothers, Chris and Shawn, went with Mom. It took two and a half hours to go over everything that Dad has to learn. The prosthesis man told Dad that there is so much more to learn (thanks, Doc!) to walk on his leg. It weighs thirty pounds, and the knee is computerized. It is very difficult to learn to walk on the fake leg! It will take Dad two weeks inside the house just to learn how to put it on and walk a little bit and then two more months or more to walk with a cane. He could fall very easily, so I will go with him every step of the way, even though his prosthesis man told him to be careful of dogs. I do not think I like him either!

Mom and Dad did not get home until eight thirty. Then Demi started pacing, panting, and acting uncomfortable. Mom was concerned that she had bloat (standard poodles are prone to this, I hear). So Mom consoled her until twelve thirty or one. She was fine. I thought she was faking because she just wanted attention. Typical Demi, the queen!

Mom and Dad both stayed home from work today because they are tired. I had to fix breakfast. Cereal and toast. I am getting quite good at cooking! I may be a chef instead of a Navy Seal.

Love,

Veni

#5

There are those days when plans simply don't work out, Veni. Your dad has something that most of us don't have, but he'll need to be patient and one day he'll be able to walk like you and me. Well, not really since we have four legs and he has just two, I mean one, well, actually two but one is fake.

You might share this observation with him, and it's a true story. A couple of years ago I was with the old man in old Monterey when a couple, a man and a woman walked by with their dog—that's one of us. To my amazement, this little fellow had lost his two back legs and was strolling alone in a harness with two wheels at the back. He seemed not to have a care in the world.

I have to say I was touched and even admiring. And you'd be, too. Now, this is not a solution for your dad, not at all. But there is a lesson here to be heeded. We all have something within us, and we just need to call upon it when we need it. That is persistence, courage, and tenacity. And I'm sure your dad will come to see he has all this and more.

And I think your job is to be his aide de camp, his watcher, and his pal. You know how to do that.

Well, I hope I don't sound like some sort of a new-age guru. I'm not that at all. I'm just a little fellow who can relate to your dilemma. I'd much rather nap this afternoon than sit here at the PC. But a friend is a friend. Try not to worry. You can be a great help to your dad just by lying at his feet.

Speaking of that, I'm about to take my midday snooze. Remember, watch for fleas.

Mr. Toby

#6

Dear Mr. Toby,

From which college did you graduate? I am still in high school and was told to go to a good military school by the warden at Soledog prison. Mom thinks that West Point is number one. Are you a physiologist, Toby? You give such good advice, but I have to say, I am still going to sue Dad's doctor!. However, you do give good advice and are a good friend!

Thanks, Toby,

Veni

#7

Dear Dad,

My mom's grandmother told her when she was a child that things in life, good and bad, always happen for a reason. I know that you have been wondering why losing a leg (a half a leg) had to happen to you. Well, I am going to tell you! I *love it* when you take your fake leg off every night because I now have a very comfy place to lie down. It could not be any better because I get to cuddle with you, Dad! You left me the perfect spot. I have not forgotten about the horrible thing that Dr. Z did, however! But in the meantime, I am taking advantage of the loss until your original leg is eventually found.

Love you, Dad!

Veni

"Dear Veni" Letters

#1

To all my dog friends,

Because my life has been full of such interesting experiences, I have decided that I am the perfect little dog to take on a new venture. You can tell me about your family problems, other dog problems, food complaints, etc. I can help you with anything! Remember, my IQ test was very high. Okay, okay! My highest mark was in mischievousness, but nonetheless, this is one of the reasons I will be ideal for your "Dear Veni" questions.

Please send photos along with a little bit about yourself. I am the perfect dog for this service also. You know how much I love boy dogs!

I will be fair with your fee also. My mom is collecting pennies for throw cans. She needs many!

Thank you,

Veni

PS: I will be waiting for your letters!

#2

Dear Veni,

You probably don't know me, but my name is Trigger. I am a silver Lab, and I may look like a Weimaraner to you but I promise I am 100 percent silver Lab. About two weeks ago, my owners went to go stay in your mom and dad's guest house. I heard that you are going to prison, but I was also in prison and it was called the kennel, a dog's worst nightmare! I was with two other dogs that I didn't even know, and they had their own doggy posse. During the night when everyone went home, they would unlock all the cages and then they would beat me up in my small little cage! I missed my owners *so* much! And when they picked me up, there were only three! Now my counting is bad, but I was sure that one wasn't there. I got over it, but a couple of days later my three owners (for now, I overheard my owners saying that the fourth one was at a camp in California, wherever that is) went somewhere and didn't come until much later with a *new* dog! Her name is Corona, and I was so happy, excited, and happy! Wait, did I already say that? Eh whatever, you know what I mean! It was an *amazing* day until this little angel on the outside releases her devil side. Now Veni, you might not know what I mean, but Corona bites my ears *so* hard that I start to cry! But my owners use that can trick that your mom uses on you, Levi, and Demi. Yup, that's right, I read your book and tell Demi to put a sock in it! Jeez, talk about drama queen! Corona *definitely* doesn't like it! I can see it in her eyes. Now ever since my owners got Corona, she is the one that gets all the attention! I am *so* jealous! But when we play, I tell her that I am the boss in a playful way. Veni, I really need some advice on how to survive this little devil, err, I mean angel. I think I hear someone coming. Gotta go, bye.

From,

Trigger

#3

I read your plea for help! I am so sorry to hear what happened to you in doggie jail. I would turn them in to the doggie chamber of commerce! I will also alert Johnnie Collieran and Christopher Doxie. They will find the dogs that beat you up and put them back in jail!

Now about the new dog, will give you a little clue as to what to do. Be nice to her because she is a girl dog! Do not make her mad! Girl dogs can be a little bitchy. This is okay to say because this is what we are called.

So, bite the bullet because she may become one of your best friends or a girlfriend perhaps. My advice, give her some of your food once in a while. This will make her happy. Offer her an apple, and throw in a little diamond for her paw. I am a girl, and I love them! I think that you will be best friends, or your new girlfriend. Keep me informed!

Veni Jackson

Personal columnist for "Dear Veni"

PS. Trigger, I can tell you are a nice boy dog. My Mom is training another dog with your name! She had to rush home to change her clothes after he lifted his leg on her. She thinks that he had been holding it for a long time because her pants were *soaked*! She thought perhaps he did this because his name was Trigger?

#4

Dear Veni,

This is Hoover. I am glad to hear that you are giving advice.

My dad says that I am smarter than you. He tells me to get the blue ball out of my toy box, and I do. If he says to get the green one, I get the green one. If he spells ball, I bring the color I like best. I will also bring him the frisbee every day at exactly four. I usually catch it eight out of ten times.

I have a great life, and I am very happy. I would like to thank your mother for all of the training lessons my dad and I had with her. I only have one problem, and if you can solve it, my dad says that you would be a smarter dog than me.

#5

Dear Veni,

I can't stand being in the car. My parents bought a second home in Lake Tahoe. It is a two-hour drive from Sacramento. I love the lake. We play ball, and I learned how to dig in the sand. My dad has a kayak, and I swim behind him. Lots of fun. When I am in the car, I am so afraid that I pant the entire two-hour drive. One time we went to Montana, and I panted for two days each way. My vet has given me many different kinds of pills. I have tried something called a calming blanket. I do not want the pill that will knock me out. So Veni, please help me if you can. You will be crowned the smartest dog if you do.

Love,

Hoover

#6

Dear Hoover,

I am so sorry to hear about your car problem! This is just plain awful! But I think I have a solution for you. Just think about this for one minute. Does your Dad do most of the driving? Mom told me that he does not see well out of one eyes. Perhaps he is not a good driver? Is he erratic? Does he take the corners too fast, especially on the way to Tahoe? It sounds like you are nervous and afraid. I have two solutions. Let your mom drive, or better yet, take a limousine, have a little doggie wine, and take some calming drops from the doggie health food store. This should solve the problem!

Love,

Veni

PS: Please keep me informed.

PPS: BTW, being smarter than me would be quite a feat. I admit that I don't do the colored ball thing. I am only interested in one green ball. It is called an apple.

#7

Dear Veni,

Thanks for your ideas. Yes, my dad is blind in one eye, but he is by far a better driver than my mother. A limo and wine sounds good. I think the only way this might work would be for you to be in the limo with me. We could cuddle and hold paws. In fact, this might even work in my dad's car. I will bring you an apple if you would come to Tahoe with me the next time I go.

Love,

Hoover

#8

Done deal! I might like the lake too. I go out and stand in the sprinklers. This is sounding better and better! I *need* a vacation!

Love,

Veni

#9

Dear Veni. I have an embarrassing problem. I eat dog poop. I don't really like it, but most everyone else around here eats it, so I figured I would give it a try. My human mom picks up several times a day. It is dark out at five in the morning when she lets us out. We are not in a kennel. She has tried mixing crushed pineapple in our food. That hasn't worked. We can't have OTC meds, as some of us are of breeding age. Mom tells me that nobody will want to date me because of my bad breath. Please *help*!

Signed,

Anonymous

#10

Dear Anonymous,

OM gosh, we have to do something about this! You are right, your dating prospects will be *very* few. You might get lucky and find a boy dog who likes the same thing, but this may cause some fighting in the household. He will try to get it before you do. This will make you mad! Then the counseling begins.

I feel that your mom should get up at 4:00 a.m., rush out with a large bottle of Tabasco sauce, do a little dousing, and then let you all out to go potty. I am sure that you would love it, Miss Anonymous!. It tastes great! You and your friends might have to rush to the water bowl, however.

I hope that you know, Miss, that this is a disgusting habit! Please try to contain yourself! Do you want to be loved or not? It is difficult for your mom any boy dog to give you a kiss with your stinky breath.

Love,

Veni

PS: After my mom's mom passed away, they inherited her miniature poodle, Pepi. Mom would rush out to clean up because he did the same thing. But you know what.? He would open the poop bag and eat it right out of the bag!. Disgusting dog, she said!

#11

Great answer, Veni! I will bark like crazy tomorrow morning at four. That will get Mom up to sprinkle Tabasco sauce around, even though there are no lights in the backyard and Mom is pretty much blind. This will be fun! Thanks for your advice. I will let you know what happens. Signed, Anonymous.

PS: Pepi's habit is disgusting! I would never eat poop out of a bag!

#12

Veni,

So now that I have returned from my tour of duty, I am finally settled in at home. I am not quite sure I fit in here anymore. There are so many rules I can't believe it. I was used to doing whatever I wanted and screaming and yelling when something didn't go my way. Other people did exactly what I wanted, but somehow Mom and Dad just won't break! I have tried everything to make them feed me only cookies and chicken. I also tried to tell them I hate dog dishes and dog crates, but they keep pushing this stuff on me. I protested for a while, refusing to eat my breakfast, but they broke me down. I was starving around here.

Mom told me I looked like a stuffed sausage in my uniform but not anymore. She says I am fit and trim now. How did this happen? Mom's friend came to visit the other day. For some reason, Mom decided to tether me to her. When her friend walked in, I went into protection mode, snarling and barking and pulling away. I threw a huge fit. Mom's friend calmly looked at me, took the tether, and forced me to do obedience with her. What is going on here? After a half hour of protesting, I found myself coming to her and eventually doing my tricks for her. No matter how hard I fought, I just couldn't believe she had me enjoying myself and relaxing. I don't know who these dog people are, but somehow they fix you even when you don't want to be fixed.

Since that day, I tried to have a small fit with my sitter. Mom and Dad went on vacay, so I acted completely freaked out when she showed up. I even growled. Mom still left me, and then I realized this sitter was in charge of me for two weeks. Now I make sure she knows I am here every day just so she doesn't forget to feed and hold me. I like her, after all.

I heard your mom is the same way mine is, like a dog guru or something. These people are dangerous. They mess with your mind. Watch out.

Chesty

#13

Dear Chesty,

You need to man up. You are a marine, after all! And you are going to Hollywood, and Gunny is not! You must be nice to everyone. No growling, lifting your lips, and complaining about your food. Marines *never* complain! And if you are a bad boy, you call my mom. She will shape you up. Now you need to apologize to everyone in your family, your doggie sitter, your brother and sister, and your parents. If you do not shape up, you may have to go to lockdown, so I suggest you change your attitude.

Thanks for writing.

Veni

Author of "Dear Veni"

PS: It is a good thing you are handsome!

#14

Dear Veni,

You don't know me. But I know of you because I was given your book for Christmas. To be honest, I prefer mysteries, adventures (have you read *Tom Sawyer*?), and books on baseball. Even so, I found your book intriguing in that you have a special insight into the minds of humans and added to that, a light, even humorous response to the foibles of our keepers. I could quote Shakespeare here—"What fools mortals be"—but I won't.

At present I share a small cottage on the Pacific Coast with a mate (one of those) who is pretty good company. We've had our challenges, but let's face it, there's no perfect arrangement. He has a comfortable bed and is an excellent sleep mate. Not much of a cook. There is nothing in the cupboard other than kibble! All in all, I like this guy.

Now to get down to the reason for this note: the fact is, I'm looking for a pen pal. My partner spends hours daily at the computer. He's a writer but not of the adventures or baseball stories that I like. So there I am beside his desk with nothing to do but sleep. Don't get me wrong, I enjoy my sleep as I'm sure you do.

Oh, I suppose I should introduce myself. My name is Mr. Toby. Let me say I'm open to most subjects. I'm liberal in my thinking, friendly (I do have a problem with cats), and compassionate. All of the aforementioned suggests that we may have something in common.

You'll find my e-mail address above. Let's not use the phones. I've always been partial to the written word. Anyway, the numbers on the phone are too small for my paws.

That's it, Veni. I look forward to hearing from you one day when you find the time. And remember: no matter what anybody says, there *are* no dog days, only endless days filled with happy puppies.

(Mr.) Toby

#15

Dear Mr. Toby,

I have been thinking about your letter for a couple of days now. You are a wonderful writer, just like your Dad. I think that you have been sleeping with one eye open!

Let's talk about the food problem. Your dad needs to add a little something of interest. Demi, Levi, and I all *love* steamed broccoli. This is what Mom adds to our food for a special treat. There are some complaints at Dad's office, however, when we eat broccoli. All the employees have to hold their noses when Demi arrives. Their comment: "Uh, she had broccoli today, right!" Leave it to Demi! Levi and I are good doggies. We are much more discreet! I need you to listen up here, Mr. Toby. Mom tries to keep us on the light side. We all must have a waist. I do not know you, but I suspect that you might be a little pudgy? Just a guess. If I am right, broccoli for you, Mr. Toby. I hope your dad knows how to cook!

Other than the food problem, I think you have a wonderful life. You are very lucky compared to some of the doggies that write me. FYI, I do not like cats either! And why, oh why do you like baseball? I like to chase a ball, but I think the game on TV is very boring. Give me the dog channel anytime!

Mr. Toby, if you will check out my book, there is a very pretty little white dog in the back of the book who is looking for a date. I would have to check out your commonalities first, of course. I want to be sure that you would be a good match for a date or pen pal. Please send a photo!

Veni Jackson

Author of *Veni, Vidi, Vici*

#16

Dear Veni,

I am in trouble again, and I desperately need your help. You don't know me, but hopefully we can meet soon. My name is Kirby, and I'm a big giant schnauzer. My sister is Chessa, and she is a standard schnauzer, so not quite as big as me, and she also minds better.

The problem is the doorbell and people coming to visit. My mom has trained me not to rush the door, but I can't help myself. I really, really, *really* need to see who is there before she opens the door, but Mom just doesn't understand my need to protect her. I would never hurt anyone (as long as they are friendly), but she still gets mad. She tells me to sit and stay, and I do (sometimes), at least sit for a minute. But it's awful and I'm so anxious I tremble, so the minute she opens the door, I push it open and check everyone out to make sure they are friendly. Now Mom is locking us up in the bedroom before she will open the door, and I worry so much. Veni, please help!

Hope to see you soon!

Kirby

#17

My dear Kirby,

This is so simple, but just a warning, you might not like it! I am afraid that I have to send this to your mom also. I just have a feeling that you may not tell her!

But just to make you feel a little better, this has been used on Demi, Levi and me. But a heads up. We try to hide them, but Mom *always* hears us, but you can try it

Your mom must get three coke cans, rinse them out well, put them on a paper towel to drain, then add exactly twenty pennies, and put some tape over just the top of the can. Then she has to raise the can above her head and pop it so it makes a very loud noise. She must not shake it. She has to pop it and say, "*No bark*!" And "*Get back*!" As soon as the doorbell rings, your mom has to have a can right where she can grab it. She must put the can behind her back, pop it, and tell you to stay back! She also to have a can *everywhere*. You know what my mom does if we are barking. She just says, "I am going to get the can!" We all get quiet. I personally *hate* that can. It is a monster!

If you are a good boy, perhaps your mom will allow you to eat the paper towel after she finishes.

Love,

Veni

#18

Dear Veni,

I have a problem, and I need your expertise. Everything I sees makes me want to go pee. I pee on pillow, and I pee on trees. I pee on the wall, and I pee on Gage's knees. I pee on a door, and I pee on the floor. I pee on my brother Sam, and I pee at the store. Oh my, oh my, what do I do? I can't help myself. Sometimes I even go poo. Please, oh please, help me, dear friend. Please, oh please, I want this to end.

Love,

Scorch

#19

My Dear Scorch,

My, oh my, oh my. You do have a problem!

I do believe that you need a good trainer, like my mom!

Perhaps your parents picked the wrong name, Scorch.

Should it have been Torch?

With this name, at least you could help stop fires

instead of lifting your leg on tires.

You had better stop this disgusting peeing,

or a doggie psychologist you will be seeing.

Your mom and dad will be spending a lot of money.

It is a good thing that they love you, honey!

Love,

Veni

Mayor of Chualar

PS: Please send a photo. I do love boy doggies!

#20

If Flynn would write a letter to Veni, this is probably what he wants to say.

Dear Veni,

I hope you're doing awesome!

I'm doing great myself. My name is Flynn. I'm a beagle. I came from a litter of six, and I was the smallest.

I also look different from my brothers and sisters. The white coat that's supposed to go around my nose is uneven. In fact, when I look at the mirror, it looks like only one side is coated with white and the other half is brown. But that's okay. My adoptive parents said that they liked my look. That's why they chose me.

I'm four years old now. When I was just a baby, my daddy's sister didn't see me going out of her room. She closed the door with a quarter of my tail still inside. Mommy said the doctor had to cut it because it got injured really bad.

I'm turning five this May. But I still don't know how to do the trick my parents have tried to teach me all these years. I bark at people and dogs. My daddy would tell me he can't get enough sleep sometimes because I bark too much. I can't seem to remember where to pee at the right spot. My daddy says it's hard to walk with me because I always run around and it burns all of his energy. But what can I do? I just can't stop myself from running and sniffing when we're out.

You're the mayor in your town. That's what I heard. You must know what I should do, right?

If you were me, what would you do?

Flynn

#21

Dear Mr. Flynn,

You really have a tail to tell, my poor Mr. Flynn!

Now to your problem area. I am just as smart as my mom because I watch her train all those unruly dogs. Of course, I am not one of them! If I were you, I would hide all the Coke cans at your home because I am going to tell you what my mom does to me when I bark. I watch her. She puts exactly twenty pennies in a clean can, puts some tape over the opening, and then she raises her hand really high (above her head), gives it one sharp shake, and says, "*No bark*!" She tries to make a statement with it!. And believe me, I *hate the can*! Mom has about five of them, so she can have them at her disposal. All she has to say to all of us now is, "I am going to get the can!" If we are really bad, she throws it at us! Demi and Levi are the worst doggies. I am a good girl! Levi has a bark collar because he barks in the car, but Mom takes the can with her also.

Mr. Flynn, you have to tell your dad that you are a beagle! As you know, your breed loves to run. This is what you were bred to do. Your dad has to find a good dog trainer like my mom and me. It is imperative that you learn to come when called! And you should not bark at other dogs and people. That is not polite! Your dad needs a whistle when you go outside and start barking—one that he can put around his neck. I am sorry to say that you will not like the noise, so just stop what you are doing and shape up!

I know that I am a little bossy, so my mom says, but you must behave yourself so you poor Dad can get some sleep. The can will be right by his bed stand. My mom gives it one really *hard* shake, so get prepared!

Veni Jackson

Mayor of Chualar

PS: Please send a photo, Mr. Flynn. I love to get photos of handsome boy dogs!

My Run for Mayor!

Letter 124

To all my human and doggie friends,

There are two very important events happening in my life as I speak. One I am very happy about, and the other makes me very sad!

Let me talk about the latter first. Mom and Dad are leaving Levi, Demi, and me for fifteen days! And guess where they are going? *To Budapest*! This is my country! I pleaded to go with them so I could see my brothers, sisters, dog mom, and human mom. They refused to take me! And to make matters worse, they are leaving Demi in charge of Levi and me. No doggie sitter! They tried to get one, but nobody wanted the responsibility of taking care of the two pumik, they said. Can you believe? They say we are too much work! And they were afraid that I would escape like I did the last time they left.

Demi will be in charge of feeding us (we *could* do this ourselves for heaven's sake!). Levi's job is cleaning dog bowls and filling water bowls. My job? Cleaning dog poop! Demi made the decisions. How sweet of her to give me this job! She hates me! All three of us will be in charge of protecting our home. We just had our teeth sharpened to prepare for any intrusion. I did try their suitcases to see if I could fit, but they were *locked*! They will be gone for fifteen days. Sniff, sniff! And I am certain I will be skin and bones when they arrive home. And *what if there are terrorists* on the plane? What will happen to us. My brother, Chris, would take Demi but not Levi and me. We would have to go to an orphanage! Boo-hoo! I hope Mom and Dad have fun!

One bit of good news just in case you did not know. I was voted as mayor of Chualar. I had 360 votes! My inauguration will be some time in the first week or two of January 2017. I have many plans for the little town of Chualar. The very first thing on the agenda will be cleaning up the town. We have many volunteers. Anyone who would like help is welcome! There are two other dogs that are mayors of little towns. I am going to call them for a doggie mayor convention. We want our towns *great again*! I will let you know the date. I hope all of you can make it! And just in case you did know and were wondering how I got elected because I was born in Hungary, the rule *does not* apply to canines!

Love,

Veni

Newly elected Mayor of Chualar

And sad Pumi!

Letter 125

Hi Veni,

I'm so proud of you and your recent victory! Keep up the great work, and I know you'll be sure to add lots of class to your office. Think of the small dogs. We will need your help also.

Woof, woof,

Toby

Letter 126

To all my friends,

It is close to the end of the year, 2016. I am now four years old. The years go by so fast! At least this is what my mom keeps saying.

I did a lot of dog training this year. I had to help Mom. Levi and I are experts now. I have learned so much in four years that I told my Mom that she can take a break, and I will take over. She said that I am so bossy that I probably could start my own training school! I am not sure if I should take this as a compliment.

I have to tell you about my favorite bone. I only get it when Mom does her exercise every day. There is only one of them. I know it is for me. Just lately, Demi (the queen) has been grabbing it before I get to the family room. She lays on the couch munching! It makes me *so* angry that I bark at Mom. I want Mom to take it from Demi. She refuses! I stare at Mom and bark. She tells me to knock it off!. So... It took a while, but I figured it out. I go to the side window and bark, which makes Levi and Demi jump down from the couch to see what is going on. I rush over and grab the bone. By the time Demi gets back to the couch, I am happily chewing. Oh... I am so smart!

This year I had to have an operation. Some veterinarian told me that I did not have nice hips! I told him that all my boy dog friends disagree. How dare he! Mom was devastated. She says I am a beautiful pumi and wanted to show me. I was not as sad. I was actually glad that I did not have to go to dog shows. Sorry, Mom!

On the good side, I did get a certificate from AKC for my HT herding title. The plan is to get started in 2017. There are other degrees that Mom has in mind for me for 2017 also. I hope she gets lots of rest! My first book, *Veni, Vidi, Vici,* got very good reviews. I know that everyone will enjoy the second book titled *Born to Lead*. I really had a lot of fun writing it!

And now for the big news in 2016. I ran for *president*—until the animal association got threatened by one of the campaign managers. They told them that if I did not drop out of the race, all the farm animals would not get food or water. Despicable!

This is when I decided to run for mayor of Chualar, California. I *am* now the newly elected mayor of Chualar, with 360 votes. My inauguration will be January 14, 2017. I am not going to sit on my rear. I plan on working my tail off

I will keep you informed,

Love,

Veni

Letter 127

Bow wow, Veni! They gave you an inch and you took a mile! You obviously know how to work your sheeple! Or maybe you did it on good looks alone. Your magic hairstyle? (Who knows?! I don't. I can't really think beyond now, soon, or just happened. I know about ten human words. My guess is you are pretty much in the same. So how did you do it!)

What were your campaign promises? I don't read papers or most of my e-mails. (Old-fashioned that way. Snail mail, sleeker mail, pee mail.) Will you free all dogs from prison on your first day in office, make afternoon snacks mandatory? Outlaw leashes? Or just take a poop and lie down?

If you're mayor, does that mean you get a chauffeur and can command humans? Do you get to pee on anything you want? Will they put up a statue of you? Wow. If you get a statue, will I be able to pee on it, or would you consider that bad form?

I'm just so impressed. People are so very dumb. Er, sorry, human, if you're reading this. Good job on getting some dog power going at the local level!

I didn't vote. I can't reach the ballots or figure out what that it means. How did you manage to get elected? It's mind-blowing. Anyway, please remember me and my after-the-fact support. I'm thinking of building some doghouses out your way. Well, thinking of it, I can't build anything. Oh, never mind. Just a passing thought. I'm going to have a nap.

Oh, I forgot to say, if you need to hire a captain of fun police, please consider me.

Just barooo! Barooo, to you!

Your old crony,

Ranger, HT PT (almost)

mover of sheep, handsome boy modeling school graduate, canine wannabe real estate developer, good pisser, and Cardiff court HOA fun patrol

Louie

Letter 128

To all my friends,

I have a favorite place that I visit almost every day. Mom trains all those out-of-control dogs there. Thank goodness, I am not one of them! It is Louie's jewelry store. Louie thinks I am beautiful, and I think he is handsome and *owns a jewelry store*! We would be the perfect match. I love diamonds, and he loves me.

But the more I think about our lives together, I see there could be a problem. What would Louie do when I am herding sheep. He is very debonair, and I am a tom girl (not that I do not love diamonds!). I visualize him watching me herd sheep. He would be sitting on a gold throne and smoking a cigar while wearing his bow tie. He will be speaking French to all the girl dogs. No. I would not be able to trust him. I am certain he would not be faithful. No, not at all!

Louie, thanks so much for the diamond collar you gifted me. Would you like me to return it? *Umm*. I think I heard you say there is no-return policy. I know you love girl dogs to look beautiful, so thank you so much for the gift! We can stay friends, right?

Love,

Veni

Thank you for offering to be my secretary of agriculture.

PS: Louie's mom, Adrianna, is on the left, and Suzanne is on the right. They work for Louie. They are squeezing me *so* hard that my ears popped straight back!

Letter 129

To all my doggie friends and human friends,

I just had the best day a doggie could ever have! On January 14, 2017, I became mayor of Chualar, California. It was my inauguration day! It took place at the Chualar Elementary School. Mom took cookies (of course I was not offered one!). About forty people were there to greet me. My mom's friend, Jayleen, got me a wonderful scarf to put on my collar that said Veni, mayor of Chualar, all in red, white, and blue. I was so proud!

I am still working on my cabinet, but I do have five doggies assigned. Johnnie Collieran will be my attorney general. As you might recall, Johnnie is my attorney. He got Demi, Levi, and me out of jail. Tippy the terrier will be the chief of police. Tippy says she can sniff out any kind of trouble! And Princess will one of my cabinet advisor. She will also be my chauffeur. And Harley, a Yorkie, will be my secretary of defense. He is one tough little hombre! And Louie will be my secretary of agriculture. He may be from France (and knows his wines) but has decided to study broccoli instead.

I would like to thank the residents of Chualar for my 360 votes. I promise to do a good job! I also promise not to sit on my rear. I will work my tail off to keep Chualar clean and inviting.

Love,

Veni

Rica and Rocco have offered to be my bodyguards, however I do not believe I need them. I can run fast and bite legs! They may be afraid of me!

Veni's bodyguards

Rica and Rocco

Chief of police

Tippy

Veni's Chaffeur

Princess

Veni's secretary of defense

Lexi

Veni's secratary of agriculture

Louie

Printed in the United States
By Bookmasters